W9-BZH-080

NRC CASS COUNTY PUBLIC LIBRARY
400 E. MECHANIC
HARRISONVILLE, MO 64701

0 0022 0610512 0

Treasure Island

BOOKS FOR YOUNG PEOPLE BY
JEWELL PARKER RHODES

Ninth Ward

Sugar

Bayou Magic

Towers Falling

Ghost Boys

Black Brother, Black Brother

Paradise on Fire

JEWELL PARKER RHODES

TREASURE

ISLAND

Runaway Gold

Quill Tree Books
An Imprint of HarperCollins Publishers

Quill Tree Books is an imprint of HarperCollins Publishers.

Treasure Island: Runaway Gold
Copyright © 2023 by Temple Hill Publishing
All rights reserved. Printed in the United States of America.
No part of this book may be used or reproduced in any manner
whatsoever without written permission except in the case of
brief quotations embodied in critical articles and reviews. For
information address HarperCollins Children's Books, a division of
HarperCollins Publishers, 195 Broadway, New York, NY 10007.
www.harpercollinschildrens.com

Library of Congress Control Number: 2023934237
ISBN 978-0-06-299835-4

Typography by David Curtis
23 24 25 26 27 LBC 5 4 3 2 1
First Edition

To Brad,
who inspires laughter, love, and joy

Fifteen men on a dead man's chest—
Yo-ho-ho, and a bottle of rum.

—Robert Louis Stevenson, *Treasure Island*

Treasure Island

Sailing Free

I tiptoe down the stairs, four flights in all, my skateboard held tight against my chest.

As soon as sunlight streamed through my window, I knew it was time to get up.

Go. Jump out of bed, dash on my clothes. Escape the house. Sneak out before Ma calls, "Zane!" Do *this*, do *that*. Endless chores.

Summer's almost gone. School hasn't begun. Adventure time.

Behind me, Hip-Hop *thunk-thunks* down the steps, his nails scratching *clickity-clack*.

"Shhh."

We pause. Hip-Hop, panting; me, listening for roomers waking.

Hip-Hop's only twenty pounds, but he's sturdy, tough. A rat terrier. Black with white patches. Brown streaks.

"Stay if you can't be quiet."

Hip-Hop whimpers, lifts his paw.

We high-five. "Deal," I say.

Tiptoe, tippy-toe, tip-toe, one last flight to go.

With any luck, Ma will be in the kitchen. Every morning before dawn, she's prepping breakfast for the tenants: kneading dough, chopping vegetables for egg scrambles, simmering oatmeal, slicing melons.

Me and Hip-Hop halt on the bottom step. My breath quickens. Two feet to freedom, then out the front door. We have to run quick. "Ready?" I whisper. "One, two . . ."

"Zane, is that you?"

Hip-Hop barks.

"Traitor," I say, then holler, "Yeah, Ma. It's me."

"Where do you think you're going?"

Ma looks like a maid. Wearing an apron, her hair pulled back. When Dad was alive, she looked softer. Sometimes, she wore earrings and lipstick. It was just us three. Now she looks worn down, always tired.

"I need you to set the table. Then see me in the kitchen."

"I promised to meet Kiko and Jack."

"You can meet them after chores."

"Aw, Ma. Skate park is going to get crowded."

"Don't argue with me, Zane." Face stern, she turns back toward the kitchen.

"This is your fault," I say to Hip-Hop. He looks ashamed. "When am I going to be a kid again? No work. Just playing. A boy and his dog."

Hip-Hop barks.

"That's what I'm talking about!"

I set plates, forks, knives, and spoons. Place water glasses, coffee cups.

Drapes closed, the house seems like a tomb.

After Dad died, Ma had to take in boarders. All of them old, smelling of Vicks VapoRub and mothballs.

Mr. Penny, carrying his false teeth in a jar, always sits at the head of the table. Reverend Thomas, between bites, murmurs prayers. His wife never says much, just eats. Or twists and shreds a paper napkin in her lap. Mr. Butler's diabetic. Retired, he stopped driving buses. He's cool, though. Sometimes he smiles, says "Good kid." Grips my shoulder. Like he knows it's hard not having a dad. Beneath the table, he sneaks sausage, chicken, even green beans to Hip-Hop, then winks at me.

I don't set a place for Captain Maddie.

"Finished."

Ma wipes her hands on a dish towel, moving toward the kitchen counter. "Take this tray upstairs."

"You sure Captain Maddie's up?"

"Yes. Earlier and earlier every day," she says, shaking her head. "Says hurricane season isn't over."

"Hurricanes?"

"She's definitely a character."

Ma doesn't say anything bad about anyone. But I know Captain Maddie tries her patience.

Captain Maddie loves giving orders like she's the boss. Owner of the house.

Her room is one floor above mine. Nights, I hear her pacing. Hear her old woman's shuffle, her cane's *thump, thump.* Sometimes, at midnight, I hear shouting, curses. Not clear if she's awake or dreaming. Sometimes, I hear frightful wailing: "Stay away, stay away." I used to listen for an answer or the footfall of another person. But Captain Maddie is always alone. Haunted by ghosts.

I lift the tray of wheat toast, grape jelly, coffee, and a hard-boiled egg.

"Zane, remind her of the rent." Worry strains, creases around Ma's eyes. "She likes you."

"Sure, Ma," I say, exiting, climbing the stairs.

I don't tell Ma I remind Captain Maddie of her dead son. "A rogue wave swept him from the ship. He was my best first mate," she often says. I always squirm, feeling sad.

Captain Maddie's been rooming here for nearly a year. When she arrived, she handed Ma a fistful of bills. But the money ran out months ago. Whenever Captain Maddie hears "money," she ignores Ma. Tells another sailing story. (Ma doesn't like begging.)

Like Ma, I don't want to be evicted, our home sold. Dad was so proud of it.

The city says Ma owes back taxes. "They just want to demolish it for apartment buildings, condos," Ma says. Already, neighbors on either side of us have sold their homes and moved away. Land values are going up. Investors pressure bankers, bankers pressure the city, and taxes rise. Everybody gets richer except us, a grieving family trying to keep a home.

It isn't fair.

I hope Captain Maddie has another stack of bills.

I climb four flights of narrowing stairs. Then one flight higher to the turret, an attic room turned into an apartment.

Knock. No answer. I knock again.

I shouldn't be here. Shouldn't be working in a run-down house filled with old people. I should be hanging out with friends, feeling wind, the fresh air.

I knock harder. Hear a grunt, then, "Enter."

The room looks like Captain Maddie's lived in it for thirty years. Maps on the wall, mounds of books stacked on the dresser, the floor. Shelves with bottles filled with blue-green liquid, jars of spices (cloves, cinnamon, and mustard) and dead, swirly things. Bugs? Baby catfish? A dead jellyfish. A Jolly Roger flag is nailed on the closet door. Though I can't figure out what's jolly about a black flag with a blistering-white skull and crossbones.

Through a telescope, Captain Maddie peers out the bay window.

I set the tray on the bed, the only uncluttered space, then stand beside her, looking out at the water.

We live in Far Rockaway, Queens, my one and only home. Far off, New York City's densely packed skyscrapers shimmer like castles in the mist. I watch rolling waves. Ships parting water.

Rockaway feels like an island, but it's actually a peninsula jutting into the Atlantic Ocean. It's beautiful. A cloudless horizon. Seagulls soaring. Blue sky and water mirroring each other.

"You can stop gaping."

I snap my jaw closed.

"You're called to it, too?"

Does she mean the ocean? Or the city? My whole life I've never walked Manhattan streets. I don't swim much. The shifting sandbar and rip currents are dangerous.

"Where's your ship?"

I frown. "What?"

"That board you sail on. The one with wheels."

"You mean my skateboard?"

Captain Maddie is tiny, walnut brown. First glance, she's somebody's harmless aunt, but her eyes pierce. Her fingers are skeletal yet strong.

I flinch as she grips my arm.

"Freedom," she whispers, hoarse. "You're called to it, too. Aren't you? That's why you sail."

I gulp.

"Wind in the sails, balancing on deck. Feeling free."

"Yes, ma'am."

"Captain, not 'ma'am,'" she rasps, her finger poking my chest. "Captain Maddie of the Turbulent Underground Sea."

How can there be an underground sea?

Her finger points up, then down. "Above and below. Water and the dead are everywhere."

I shiver. I think Captain Maddie's crazy. A cross between a witch and a pirate.

Shifting closer, I try to see what she sees. Water topped with foam. Sunlight making rainbows. Bent, she frowns, twisting the knob, refocusing her telescope.

"Look," she says, stepping back.

Strangely, the telescope is aimed past the water, the motorboats, sailboats, yachts, and pontoons. Captain Maddie's obsessed with land. Manhattan. I don't understand.

"Been everywhere," she says softly, her gaze unfocused. "Sailed from Benin, the coast of Africa. Climbed in rank. Sailed through Oceania. The Caribbean. The Pacific route of Captain Cook."

"Why'd you sail here?"

Suspicious, she barks, "Why do you care? What's your business?"

I stumble back. She's the fearsome captain now. On a ship, she could order me to walk the plank. Drop and drown.

Captain Maddie grips her cane; its handle, two ivory snakes curling around wood. It's creepy. Two thick, curved throats. Four eyes, beady-black, spying; two forked tongues, ready to strike.

I shiver. Like a current shifting, her expression calms. "Saint Lucia," she murmurs, wistful.

I relax. I've heard this tale before.

"Me and my boy found treasure. Silver candelabras. Gems."

"Rubies?"

"Yes. And gold-plated goblets and diamond-crusted mirrors. We dredged a hidden harbor. Not deep enough to sail my ship. But just right for a small boat and oars."

This is the Captain Maddie I like best. Voice, warm; eyes, bright. St. Lucia is my favorite adventure. Discovering bounty on a volcanic island.

"Tell me again about the sea turtles."

"A foot wide and three feet long. Their shells a glorious splattering of green."

"They watched you?"

"Yes." She smiles. "They swam by and between us as we dove, bringing silver and pearls to the rocky shore."

"Whose treasure was it?" I ask, knowing the answer.

"Conquistadors!" Captain Maddie cackles. "You like my stories, Zane?"

"Yes! Then a French pirate—"

"Jambe de Bois."

"Named for his wooden leg!"

"Sunk the Spanish galleon, claimed the treasure."

"Hundreds of years ago. The 1500s, right?"

"Yes. Treasure was meant to be shared. His second-in-command mutinied, rallied a small crew to steal it. Jambe de Bois outwitted them. He hid it—him and his new first mate. They went into hiding. Some say they sailed as far as Cape Horn. Eventually, they were found."

Her voice lowers. "The black spot."

"What's the black spot?"

She never tells.

"Neither got to live out their days. Both ambushed and killed." Her brow creases. "But they never spoke the secret. Didn't tell." Hands trembling, she turns toward the window.

I follow her gaze. What's she looking at? The water? The distant skyscrapers? Or nothing at all? Her eyes are fixed, glazed.

"So, how'd you find the treasure?" I say, distracting her.

She claps gleefully. "I found the map."

"Where?" I shout, knowing full well where.

9

"An outdoor market in Parrot Bay. A pretty young girl with hoop earrings thought it a silly drawing. An imaginary world. Time dulled memories. I purchased it for pennies. Jambe de Bois, Pirate Peg Leg, had been forgotten."

"But not by you! You're good at finding treasure."

"Yes, yes, I am," her voice rises, then breaks. "Captain Maddie—Captain Maddie—"

I chime, "Of the Turbulent Underground Sea!"

Quick, she steps close, her finger poking my chest. I flinch.

Storytime is over. Her stare unnerves me.

"You remember what I told you?" she snaps. "Do you, Zane?"

"Yes. Watch for any strangers."

"What else?"

"Especially seafaring men," I parrot.

"Or boys," she shrieks. "Seafaring boys."

This is stupid, I think, shuffling backward toward the door.

"Blackbirds look back," she moans, her palms pressing against the window.

(Blackbirds? Not in Rockaway.)

Her emotions shift. "Mutineers. Scurvy lowlife." Angrily, she swings, stabs the tip of her cane like a sword.

"Boundless greed. Some treasures better forgotten than stolen," she says, pacing, bellowing. "Two-faced. Wanting tribute from the dead. Two-faced men like—"

I don't catch her last words. Captain's ranting, garbled.

Got to go! I think. *Gotta get out of here.* Creeping backward, I blurt, "Captain Maddie. Rent's due."

She spins, glaring at me. Then screeches, "Get that rat dog out of here."

Hip-Hop, sitting in the doorway, barks. Juts his head, growling.

"I keep a clean ship. No rats here." Wild-eyed, cane flailing, Captain Maddie stomps forward.

"Come on, Hip-Hop."

He ignores me, dashing, leaping onto the bed.

"Hip-Hop, nooooooooo."

Captain Maddie swats her cane, but Hip-Hop's quick. Carrying a slice of toast, he flies off the bed and out the door.

I run, too.

Captain Maddie curses, pounding her cane on the floor.

I hear Ma yelling, "Zane! What's going on? Zane!"

Down a flight, then another. Rushing, leaping.

Boarders fling open their doors.

"What's going on?" In night robes, Reverend Thomas

11

and his wife peek out their door. "Sin ye not," the reverend scolds. "Spare the rod, spoil the child."

"I didn't do anything," I yell back.

Hip-Hop sets his toast down and barks. "Run for it," I holler, and he does, gripping the bread as he races down another flight.

I climb onto the staircase rail, sliding, sailing down another flight. I pass Mr. Penny, his gums flapping without his teeth. Mr. Butler cheers. "Never mind the old bat!" he shouts, looking upstairs while Captain Maddie screams like she's lost a treasure.

Hands on her hips, Ma's scowling at the stairwell bottom.

"Ma," I plead, my hand on the doorknob. "Pleeeease." I give her my cutest smile.

Hip-Hop gulps the toast in three bites.

Ma laughs and nods.

I jump to the floor, grip my skateboard, and fling open the door. Light floods our dark house.

"Be back by dinner," calls Ma.

I smile, wave. "Come on, Hip-Hop—we're free."

We both leap, dive off the porch, then keep running. Running, running. Far enough away, I stop running and look back.

Captain Maddie is at the window. *Can she see me?*

She's a sentry keeping watch. Looking due north.

Waiting for a storm, I think. Strangers approaching. Not from sea but from land.

I frown, confused. A bit frightened.

Maybe Ma *should* evict her?

I stoop, patting Hip-Hop's head. "You could've grabbed a slice for me."

We walk into town. Boardwalk shops are mostly shuttered. Wind has knocked down signs. Trash—napkins, popcorn bags, and the twisted white paper rolls for cotton candy—litters the walk. Opening early, the corn dog man rolls up his store's aluminum slats. He waves.

"Hi, Mr. Cohen. Save me one."

"You bet, Zane."

I set my board down. Push off, goofy style, my right foot forward on deck, my left leg stroking backward.

I'm off. Sailing the boardwalk. The boarded wharf and stalls fly by. "Free!" I scream. Hip-Hop runs beside me. "Free!" Out of the house. Air rushing over me. Balancing my body. Knees bent, keeping it loose. No worries. My whole self relaxes.

I lift my head, smelling salty air, seaweed, and mucky sand. Then, head low, I grip, making my feet like magnets, lifting the board into the air, leaping off the boardwalk and into the street. A car swerves; a man honks angrily.

"Sorry." I do another ollie—leaping onto the curb.

I grin. "C'mon, Hip-Hop. Let's go."

We both take off. My legs steadily kicking, stroking the sidewalk. Hip-Hop's small, powerful legs match my wheels. We're both smiling.

There's a rush of adrenaline. My body switches to high gear, leaning like a sprinter. Core tight, muscles taut, I'm in control. *Rush.* Heading north. Commanding the board, using my body weight to balance, shift the deck's direction.

"Cruise," I holler. Hip-Hop slows his gait.

Captain Maddie's right. I'm free sailing. Steering my own fate.

I zigzag once, twice, then shift sideways, carefree, coasting, my arms spread wide.

"Zane!" Kiko waves from the park.

"See you've got your helmet," I yell. You can't miss it—it's yellow, a too-bright, hurt-your-eyes yellow.

"Yeah. Brought a spare for you," she answers.

Pushing down sharply on the board's tail, I stop. "Thanks."

Hip-Hop prances about Kiko.

"Some serious tricks today. Right, Hip-Hop? Here." She offers the helmet. Matching yellow.

Kiko knows I can't afford a helmet. She can. (Her dad's a doctor. Her mom's an Africana Studies professor. This summer she's teaching in Ghana.)

Kiko always has spare helmets for me and Jack. She doesn't embarrass us. Says she keeps them for when her cousins visit. She doesn't know we know she doesn't have any cousins. We asked Dr. Kitaji.

"Seen Jack yet?"

"He'll be here." Looking down the street, she squints, frowns. "His dad is back."

I groan. Jack's dad is a long-haul trucker. It's always better when he's gone.

Worried, too, I start looking for Jack. Since second grade, I've known the pattern. Dad home, Jack had accidents. Bruises, sprains. A black eye; sometimes two. "Clumsy," he'd say. None of the teachers figured it out. Or if they did, they didn't say or do anything.

I scan the park. I know all the skaters. Neighborhood friends since elementary. But no Jack.

There's Jenny, who's great at pop shove-it, spinning her board easily beneath her feet. Dylan and Teddy both love speed and swing high, up and down, between the skate bowl's crest and bottom. Malcolm practices heel scrapes and powerslides.

Off in the distance, I see a new guy, tall, lanky, gliding on his board. But no Jack.

I whistle.

Nothing.

I whistle again. The last note trilling high, hanging in the air. Again.

A whistle—low, sustained—answers me.

"There!" shouts Kiko, pointing.

I smile, relieved, then catch myself, my lips tight.

Jack's skating slow, his body tilting left while his hand holds his side.

"His dad still thinks he's a punching bag." Furious, Kiko skates off. At the bowl's rim, she looks back at me, fierce. Then tips her board, rolling down into the pit.

"Hey, Jack."

"Hey." Defiant, gazing at me straight, he dares me to say something about his bruised face.

"Watch me nail a kickflip."

"You wish." Jack grins. Kickflip is his specialty. He's the best skater of us all.

I keep loose, roll into the skate bowl, letting myself rise, then fall, rise, then fall like a pendulum. Curving the sides helps me pick up speed, rise higher and higher above the rim. At the highest point, my body parallels the bowl's bottom. Kiko and the other skaters watch atop the bowl, respecting my attempt.

Focus. I keep my eyes fixed on where I want to go.

My breathing slows. Swooping through air, my board lifts toward the clouds.

Now. Sailing upward, I reach down, grip my board in the middle, between the wheels. Then I let go, my feet losing connection, and I try to flip the board counterclockwise. My hands fly outward, and I start to fall. Feels like forever . . . a slow-motion roll toward the concrete bottom. I hear Kiko screaming. Others shouting.

The board slams first. Then me, onto my right side. My head next, skidding on concrete.

I'm stunned. Breath's been slammed out of me. I hear fellow skaters clapping, calling encouragement. Jack yelling, "Next time." Kiko demanding, "You okay?"

My right shoulder aches. "I meant to do that."

Hip-Hop, peering down into the bowl, whimpers.

"If that's as good as you've got, you should just lay there."

I look up to my left. With the sun a harsh, bright background, I see only shadows. Squinting, I shade my eyes. Tall, looming, a boy with platinum-colored hair stands, his skateboard propped on its tip. "Loser!"

"Not cool," shouts Kiko.

Sneering, the kid shrugs.

He's not from Rockaway. He's dressed in black pants, black T-shirt. Even his board is black. He spins it on its edge. A white graphic, shadow and contrast, on the deck's top, twirls by.

"Show me if you can do better," I holler, hobbling up.

"Yeah," "Come on," "Dare you," "Do it," my friends clamor. Hip-Hop growls.

"Got nothing to prove to losers," he mocks, snaking his fingers through his hair. Then cooler than ice, he jumps two-footed on his board, kicks, and coasts away.

He's right. I'm a loser. I can never land the hard tricks. One-upped.

I skate, roll upward onto and off the rim.

"Don't mind him," says Kiko, holding a squirming Hip-Hop.

I pat his head; he licks my hand.

"What a jerk. If I wasn't hurt, I would've shown him," says Jack.

"You're the best of us, Jack."

Even with a cheap, lousy board, Jack does tricks no one else can.

All three of us—me, Kiko, and Jack—hover at the bowl's rim watching neighbor kids skate. No one recognizes or even cares about the new kid.

We're all so happy to be outside, skating.

"Watch for any strangers." Captain Maddie's warning echoes. Maybe she's not crazy?

My stomach cramps. *What if he's the seafaring boy? Smirking, starting trouble?* I've got to get home. Check.

I unbuckle the helmet, hand it to Kiko. "Thanks. You saved me."

"Always. Got your back. Yours, too, Jack." She pauses. "That's why I'm telling my dad about your bruises."

"Kiko, no." Jack's face twists with fear. "He'll be gone soon enough."

"Didn't he break your arm last year?"

"You'll make things worse."

Shrugging, Kiko leaps on her board, disappearing into the bowl.

Jack clutches my arm. "Talk to her."

"I will, Jack." (Though I think Kiko's right.) "Gotta get home."

Worry is overwhelming me. By now the seafaring boy could be cruising beyond the park, down the boardwalk, passing the corn dog stand, just blocks from home.

"Let me go, Jack."

"My pop will kill me if Dr. Kitaji finds out."

Jack's panicking. I'm panicking, too, about the stranger.

Who knows what the dude might do? Ma's home. No one to protect her. What if she got hurt?

I pull away, ignoring Jack's surprise and disappointment.

"Sorry. Gotta go now. Explain later."

I thought "strangers" was a joke. Maybe it's not?

I feel dread, remembering how the strange kid seemed to like towering over me. Like a shadow over Rockaway.

Hip-Hop's fur rises.

"You feel it, too?"

I step onto my board, kicking with all my might. Fast. Faster, faster.

"Zane," Jack calls.

I don't stop. Don't turn. Don't answer.

Dad always said: "Protect your mother."

The front door is thrown open. The boarders are squawking, staggering. It looks like a bomb has hit the dining room. Broken plates, shattered glasses, oatmeal, soft eggs, and crushed toast are on the floor.

"Ma? Ma? Ma!" I scream, scared.

Mr. Butler points upward.

I dash two steps at a time. Flight one, flight two . . . all the way to the narrowest stairs leading to Captain Maddie's room.

"Ma!"

"I'm okay." Ma's kneeling beside Captain Maddie. "Help me lift her."

I reach beneath Captain Maddie's arms. She's dead-weight, passed out cold. I grunt. Ma holds her feet.

We lift her onto the bed.

"What happened?"

"Don't know. That nasty boy came in frightening our guests, tearing up the place. Demanding to see Captain Maddie."

"What for?"

"Not a clue."

Captain Maddie stirs. "My cane?" she asks, alarmed. "My cane?"

"Here." I lay the cane on the bed.

She clutches its ivory-headed snakes, then lies back, her chest heaving.

"Stay with her, Zane," Ma orders. "I'll call the doctor."

"Don't want a doctor," Captain growls after Ma's gone.

Lying on the bed, the cane across her chest, she seems so frail. Alone.

"You might have a concussion, Captain Maddie."

Captain Maddie squeezes my hand hard. I wince.

I can't move. Her eyes have a special power. Or maybe I'm just feeling sorry for her?

"I need a first mate. Quick, now. Come close."

I tilt my ear toward her mouth.

"My time's almost over."

"No, you'll be fine," I cry, pulling back. "Dr. Kitaji will help."

"Hush. Listen. I've been given the black spot. They'll come for me."

"Who? Who gave it?"

Captain Maddie sighs, wan, weary. "The others, the pirate crew."

I feel a chill. Her eyes seem to stare beyond, through

me. I turn, worried someone is really there. *Some spirit, a presence in the bedroom?* I shiver.

"A pirate's lot is hard," she says, hoarse. Her eyes fix on me. "Bounty is meant to be shared, Zane. But I stole it."

"Like a mutineer?"

"Had to." Tears flood her eyes. "No choice."

"Give it back," I urge, confused, feeling her grip weaken.

"Had to." She turns on her side, cradling the cane. "Black spot. Everyone dies."

"No," I beg softly. "Survive. I don't want to lose you."

"Are there times to be disloyal, Zane? Are there?"

I swallow. My throat's dry. I grip the headboard. Dad said a man's word was more important than gold. Disloyalty, always wrong.

Before I can answer, Ma enters, carrying a tray. "Dr. Kitaji will be here in ten minutes. Water?"

She shakes her head, murmuring, "Ghosts shall rise."

Ma sets a pitcher and a bowl on the nightstand.

My heart races. Captain Maddie quiets, her breath shallow, eyes closed.

Ma pours water into the bowl, then lifts a damp cloth, wrings and places it on Captain Maddie's wrinkled brow.

Ma did the same for Dad. At first, we thought Dad had a virus. Only Ma, wearing a mask, could nurse him. But whatever Dad had, it was slower, wasting like something breaking, bleeding inside. Dr. Kitaji said, "Without hospital tests, I can't diagnose."

Dad didn't want to go. "I'll be fine," he said. "Just need rest and my wife's stew. I'll be fine."

Reluctant, Ma agreed.

"Zane-boy, I'm strong."

Quicker than lightning, his appetite faded, his breathing strained.

The final day, he never moved. He never opened his eyes. Or said goodbye.

I turn away. I don't want to see Captain Maddie fading. Just Captain Maddie roaring, cursing. Complaining. Living. Sharing tales of her derring-do. Encounters with sea monsters. Glowing fish. Giant octopi. Whales swallowing giant sharks. Skeletons from storms, shipwrecks, tangled in kelp or buried in sand. Hunting for sunken ships in the Atlantic, the Indian Ocean. Decoding treasure maps.

"What's your latest treasure?" I'd ask. "Did you find it before you came here?"

She never said. Only exhaled, saying gravely, "During the blackest nights when the sky and ocean blend and you can't tell where one begins or the other ends, *listen.*

"Water shows the way."

I unlock, push open the windows. Outside, it's all airy and light. A breeze wafts. The ocean air soothes.

Behind me, shadows and smells of Ma's worry and Captain Maddie's fear.

I look down. On the sill is a square white card. I pick it up, turn it over. A black spot. A round, dense darkness.

My stomach cramps; my hands tremble. *The black spot.* I get it. Captain Maddie's been found. Hunted down. (But she doesn't have to die, does she?)

As if she knew I held the card, Captain Maddie, hysterical, roars, "Black spot. Black spot. Black spot."

I drop the card.

"Captain Maddie, Captain Maddie," Ma tries to soothe, smoothing her tangled hair.

More frightful moans. "Zane," she screeches as if only I could save her.

I rush to her side.

"First mate."

On my knees, I murmur, "Sssh, Miss Maddie. Please."

"Captain," she gasps, clutching my hand, marshaling her strength. Not cowering, weak, she balances on her elbow, her face close to mine, defiant in a storm.

"I'm still Captain. Beware the two-headed snake, Zane."

"There's no such—"

"Don't talk about what you don't know," she snarls. Clutching my hands, she presses her face close to mine.

I can't escape. Her amber eyes, flecked with black, compel.

"You're the first mate now. Sail on that board of yours. Find the treasure."

Treasure?

"Riches, unimaginable. Keep it safe."

A treasure to help Ma? Save our home? My pulse quickens.

"They'll be coming for it."

"It's here?" I look about the room, seeing everything in a new light—the overstuffed boxes, chests, duffel bag. I imagine coins stuffed behind books, glass vials. A treasure, here? Or beneath the mattress? Hidden in the closet?

My thoughts swirl, imagining no boarders. Ma, less tired, reading a book in the garden. Me, swerving on the sleekest skateboard. Hip-Hop, settled in a soft, furry bed, eating bones.

"Sundown, they'll come. Demanding the treasure map."

"Map?"

"She's delirious, Zane," Ma says. "Just humor her."

"What should I do, Captain?"

"Set sail, Zane. You'll need to set sail. There's no time to wait." Her voice breaks, fades. "I did my best. Protect it. Don't let them find you. Keep the treasure safe." Her eyes close. "Find . . . the wall . . . of tears."

I lay my ear to her chest.

"Is she alive?" Dr. Kitaji, carrying his medical bag, stands in the doorway. Kiko is behind him.

I stand. "Yes."

Doctor Kitaji hurries to the bedside. Ma hovers.

I tug Kiko out of the room, down the hallway, pulling her down onto the top stair step.

"Treasure," I whisper.

"What?"

"When Captain Maddie arrived, she gave Ma a fistful of bills. There must be more."

We cringe, hearing a fearful scream—a cross between pain and rage. Another. Then another. Curses. Captain Maddie, demanding, "Stay away. Stay away from me."

"If she'd found a treasure, why didn't she spend it, Kiko? She could've been living in luxury instead of here."

"Maybe the treasure's not real?" Kiko's brows lift, reminding me to be sensible.

(Yeah, I know. Pirate treasure in Rockaway? Queens? Ridiculous.)

Yet I can *feel* Captain Maddie's truth. *Feel* her guilt, her sadness despite knowing she felt she had to hide the treasure. Mysterious. None of it makes sense. Just as it doesn't make sense I'm living in a world without Dad. Yet I am.

"Zane." Ma's head pokes out the doorway. "Calm her, please."

"Me?"

"Hurry. Says you're her first mate."

I rush into the room, startled by Captain Maddie upright, flailing a small knife, slicked with blood.

Dr. Kitaji, his stethoscope dangling from his hand, hangs back.

"I cut him. I did, Zane. Cut him good."

Alarmed, I look at Dr. Kitaji.

He shakes his head. "I'm fine."

Uneasy, I inch closer.

"Put away the knife, Miss Maddie," he says firmly.

"Be careful, Zane," urges Ma. Then begs, "Maddie, please, put down the knife."

Captain Maddie ignores them, focusing on me. Eyes bright, intense, she's willing me forward, hypnotizing me.

"Calm down, Captain," I soothe. "Please calm down."

"I cut him."

"Who, Captain?" To my left, I see Dr. Kitaji filling a syringe.

"Rattler. The boy, Rattler. White hair like a ghost."

I frown, thinking of the sneering boy, taunting, laughing, looking down at me from the skate bowl's rim.

"Captain, please, put the knife down."

She stares at the bloodstained steel. Opening her hand, she lets it fall to the floor.

"Tonight, they'll come, Zane. You've got to be ready." She grips her cane, holding it across her chest like a barrier. "I'm done for, Zane.

"Protect the bounty."

"I will."

"I broke the pirate code," she says mournfully. Quick, she swings her cane as the doctor tries to administer sedation. "Leave me be," she wails. Then she twists back toward me, her nails digging into my shoulders.

"He'll come, Zane. The evilest of them all. He tracked me down like I'm scullery crew. Finally found me. Remember, the past is never past.

"Zane." She pushes the cane at me; I flinch, edging back. "Take it."

"Do it," Ma pleads.

I clutch the cane.

Sighing, Captain Maddie falls back against the pillow. She smiles, beautiful. Content.

We're all thrown off course. Me, Kiko, Ma, and Dr. Kitaji are all shocked by how relaxed she seems. Even her voice is silky soft.

"I knew I could count on you, Zane. Another time,

we would've gone journeying." She waves Dr. Kitaji away. "Don't need that shot. Have my best medicine.

"Zane, keep focused on the horizon. Steer true."

I nod.

"Say it."

"Steer true."

"Honor the bones people, whether buried in water or earth. Dead don't stay dead. Honor the bones."

"I don't understand."

Amazingly, she begins to sing, her voice steady, like the rhythm of the sea:

Safe and sound at home again, let the waters roar, Jack.
Safe and sound at home again, let the waters roar. . . .

"Sing with me, First Mate."

I hum, sputter out of tune, "Let the waters roar, Jack." (That's all I know.)

Her soprano soars:

Now we're safe ashore, Jack.

She jerks upright. "My mates. Do you see them, Zane?" She clutches my shirt. "My old shipmates."

I don't see anyone. Just Ma, Dr. Kitaji, and Kiko.

"Rest, Captain Maddie. Lay back."

She grips my shirt tighter. Her voice grows louder; her face shines with joy.

Don't forget your old shipmate.
Faldee raldee raldee raldee rye-eye-doe.

She gasps, the last note choking in her throat. Veins rise, hard and thick, along her brow and neck.

"She's having a stroke," says the doctor.

Her face twists into a fearful grimace. Looking at me, she exhales. "Take the water road. Set sail, Zane. Discover the bones." Her right eye and cheek sag. "Listen." Her voice slurs. "Waterfall. Tears."

"I don't understand."

Dr. Kitaji rushes forward, pushing me aside, taking her pulse, beginning CPR.

I drop the cane. It rolls, rattles on the floor.

"Please, please don't die. Please, Captain Maddie."

She never revives.

We all hear the final, light rattle of air.

"Nothing could've been done," says the doctor, his hands lifting off the lifeless body. "The shock was too much for her. Probably an aneurysm."

"Poor woman, poor woman," murmurs Ma.

I run from the room, collapsing on the top steps. Second death I've seen.

"Hip-Hop!" He comes running. I hold him close, my face buried against his fur.

Quiet, Kiko sits beside me.

Sounds drift from the room.

"Any family?"

"I believe she was alone. Poor woman."

"I'll call the coroner."

Ma cries. I want to cry, too. Poor Ma. Nothing is how it used to be. Strangers living in her house. Violence and death. None of this would've happened if Dad was alive.

"Let's go, Kiko." Dr. Kitaji, though not tall, towers above us. His hair, like Kiko's, is the blackest black. His expression always seems calm; his black eyes, intent. Kiko says he's good at martial arts. I didn't believe her until, one day, I saw him teaching her.

"Dad, can I stay?"

I feel Dr. Kitaji studying me. I don't look up. He saw me break down, cry when Dad died.

He pats Kiko's head. "One's spirit never dies."

I lean forward, my arms crossed over my chest. Dr. Kitaji said the same words when Dad died. Me and Kiko both scoot sideways as he passes, stepping slow. Ma squeezes my shoulder, follows Dr. Kitaji, murmuring, "I'll see you out."

Kiko doesn't say a word. She's a good friend. She knows me.

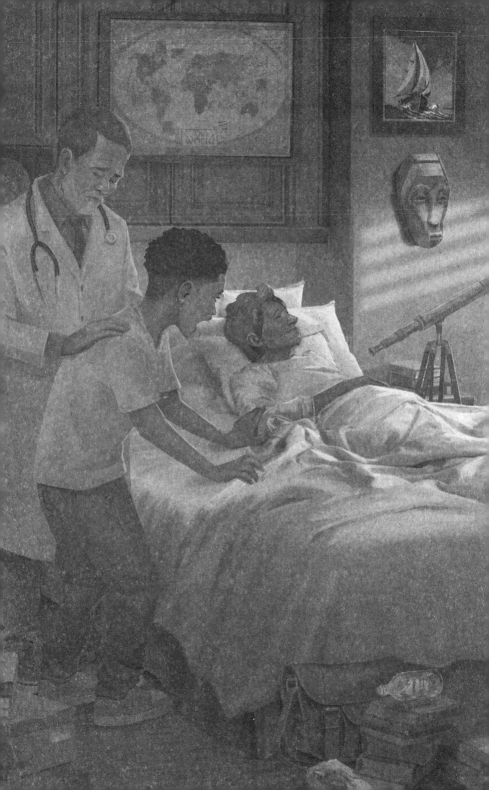

We sit—our legs, arms, shoulders still squished together. My head leans against the wooden rail. I cradle Hip-Hop, curled in my lap.

It's unbelievable how a person's alive, then not. All year, Captain Maddie must've felt so alone, afraid of discovery.

My hands clench, anger builds. Hip-Hop's ears rise.

"Rattler," I breathe.

"Who's he?"

"At the skate park. The kid who laughed at me."

"Stupid jerk."

I grin. "Don't let your father hear you say that."

Playful, Kiko elbows me.

My smile slips. "Treasure, Kiko. He was looking for treasure."

"Maybe it's true," says Kiko. "Real."

We both clamber up, eager to search.

I cross the threshold. I can't help but look toward the bed. I exhale, grateful the blue comforter covers all of Captain Maddie. Everything else is in disarray. Storm-swept.

"Rattler tore up everything."

Glass cracks under Kiko's sneakers.

"Careful."

I lift books (*The Voyage of the Beagle*, *History's Famous Women Pirates*, *Kon-Tiki*) off the floor, rummage through a cracked chest filled with ocean maps, pens, pencils, a compass, and old-fashioned navigation tools. I flip through a journal with an embossed cover: *Ship's Log*. There are handwritten lists of crew, cargo, and food. All useless. Sections filled with longitude and latitude, marking journeys around the world. (Captain Maddie didn't lie.) The back flap is signed: *Maddie Adabyo, Captain.*

Closing my eyes, I think I see her. Not dead. Not old, growling, and grumpy. But young, happy, and strong.

"Do you think this used to be real?"

I open my eyes.

Kiko's dangling a stuffed parrot by its tail.

"You mean alive? Maybe. Yes. Probably."

Hip-Hop sniffs beneath the desk.

Clothes—fancy scarves, dresses, but mainly cotton pants and leather shirts ripped from hangers, are piled on the floor.

Across the room, Kiko lifts the lid of a silver jewel box. "It's a waltz. 'The Blue Danube.'"

Kiko knows—she takes piano lessons. The tinkling music makes me sadder.

"I don't think there's any treasure, Zane."

I scan the room—objects from Captain Maddie's life are scattered everywhere. The skull-and-crossbones flag. A linen sailor's jacket. Jewels—fake or real, I can't tell. Her telescope. Captain Maddie was crafty, secretive. "She said Rattler would be back."

"'They'll'—"

"What?"

"She said, '*They'll*' be back." Kiko stands, solemn. We shiver.

Why come back if Rattler found what he was looking for?

I see the threatening card, faceup, on the floor. Near it—likely thrown against the wall—are binoculars. The case is empty, open. A binocular barrel is cracked, dented.

I undo the lens covers, peering through the eyepieces. Darkness. No streams of images, light. I turn the focus wheel. Still dark.

Not once did I ever see Captain Maddie use binoculars. It was always the telescope, now abandoned beneath the window without its stand.

Why wouldn't she have used binoculars, too? Where had they been? The closet? A drawer? In the wooden chest?

I study the glass lenses. Not a splinter of cracked glass. The binoculars should work. Using them, Captain wouldn't have had to stoop, curve her spine.

"The cane, Kiko. Get me the cane." With the cane's handle, I hit the binocular's plastic tubes again and again. They splinter, crack.

"Look. No inside mirrors." Just a roll of bills. "Hundreds." Two rolls. Each twirled tight and held by a rubber band.

"The binoculars were fake," Kiko says, surprised. "They must've never worked."

"This must be Captain's treasure. Must be thousands. Got to show Ma. Come on, Kiko." I grab the binoculars. She, the cane.

On the floor, I see the black spot. I stuff it into my pocket.

At the doorway, I stop, turn. Such a small shape. When Captain was alive, her personality overwhelmed the room. "Rest in peace, Captain."

I swear I hear "No peace."

Devil You Don't Know

Ma took eleven hundred dollars.

"That's what I'm owed. No more, no less. The police can figure what to do with the rest," Ma insists, cleaning the kitchen while Captain lies dead upstairs.

"Let me help."

"No, you and Kiko stay outside. Fresh air. Kids need it. You need it."

Then Ma hugs me tight. Trembling, she pulls away, trying not to let me see her wipe her tears. "Go on."

Kiko pulls my T-shirt, and, reluctant, I follow her outside, onto the porch.

"We need Jack."

Startled, I look at Kiko.

Her brows lift beneath her black bangs. "'*They'll*' be back."

I look out, across the street. Right now, it's empty: no tourists, neighbors walking dogs, or kids jumping rope.

But like a ghost-shadow, I can still see Rattler. Tall, slim, dressed in black. I imagine a crew of Rattlers circling.

My tongue feels thick in my throat. I didn't *see* anything. But how do I explain a mean kid taunting me? How just seeing him unnerved and frightened me?

"R-rattler," I stutter. "Rattler attacked Captain Maddie."

"Who's Rattler? Captain Maddie?" asks Jack, coming up the steps.

I feel dumbstruck again.

"What's up?"

We clasp hands, pull each other close, our arms embracing each other's backs.

Kindergarten, Jack bit me, leaving marks on my arm. I hit him with my Tonka truck. We've been friends ever since.

"Captain Maddie died," Kiko says.

Jack's brows rise. "Your boarder?"

"Yeah. Captain Maddie. She said she 'sailed all the seven seas.'"

"You believe her?" asks Jack.

I want to.

The screen door bursts open. EMTs carry a stretcher with a zippered body bag. Wordless, Ma and the boarders swarm the porch.

Hip-Hop runs beside the captain's body. He sits as

the stretcher is lifted into the van. Doors are slammed shut. The vehicle pulls away. No sirens. No emergency. Hip-Hop howls just the same. Over and over and over again.

I feel so sad.

Jack, his board cracking against concrete, starts practicing hardflips. Kiko swings the cane, aiming it, posing like it's a kendo sword.

"Show some respect," shouts the reverend. "Amen, amen," repeats his wife. Mr. Penny, without his teeth, smacks his gums in disapproval.

"Leave the kids alone." Mr. Butler winks.

Ma ushers the elders inside.

I pace, frowning.

Jack and Kiko watch me. They know I'm winding up. *Pace, pace, pace.* Muttering to myself. Hating how hard my life is. Dad dying. Ma lonely. Me lost without Dad. Us getting poor. Boarders complaining. Demanding to be served. Hate them all. (Okay, not Mr. Butler.)

Mostly, I hate how small my life is.

Captain Maddie was special, different. Wild, mysterious. Strange, I always *felt* she had lots and lots of stories, amazing adventures. In time, I believed I'd hear them all. Now there isn't any time.

Pace, pace, pace.

Kiko, holding the cane at her side, sweeps, snatches

it upward. Sunlight makes the handle glint. Two-headed snake. *What's it mean?*

My stomach aches.

Jack, flailing, keeps trying to skate down the porch steps. Again and again. Wheels rumble and clank.

"Jack, just stop it," I shout, annoyed. "And Kiko, stop pretending you're a Japanese swordsman."

"Swordswoman, duh."

Jack's board flies out from under him, crashing upside down.

"Stop. Both of you."

Kiko throws the cane. "Keep it. It's not any good."

I catch it. Kiko's right—it's too light. Not enough heft! Lousy as a sword. Lousy for stability. Puzzled, I turn the cane every which way—*tap-tap* the bottom on the porch.

"What is it?" asks Kiko.

Kiko and Jack draw close.

"Cover me. I don't want anyone to see."

We all crouch. I grip the handle. Hip-Hop sniffs.

I twist the snake head, left, then right. Then I twist harder, feeling give. Twist again and pull. The head drops off, rattles on the wood.

"It's hollow," I breathe. "Like the binoculars."

"Money?" asks Kiko.

"No, something else." I coax out a tube of ribbed

paper with a frayed edge. I lay it down and unroll it. Helping, Kiko gasps.

Jack snaps, "You kidding me?"

"A treasure map," I whisper, awed.

Squiggly lines, like waves, fill the edges of the brown paper. Turning the map upside down, it looks the same. A landmass surrounded by water.

"An island," says Jack.

"Like St. Lucia." I trace the shape. "Islands are awesome for hiding treasure."

"It's Manhattan, I think," says Kiko. "Not like today. Long ago. The land's narrow like a peninsula, but the scale seems off."

"Someone drew waves," I say, pointing. "But if this is Manhattan, they show the Atlantic but don't name what must be the East River"—I point—"Hudson, or Harlem Rivers."

"Yeah," says Jack. "It's kind of a stupid map. Rockaway doesn't even exist."

Kiko sighs. "It's an old map, Jack. Really, really old. Look at the stains, at how thin the paper is."

"So, you're an expert?" sneers Jack.

I ignore them, hovering my palms over the map. "Captain Maddie was always looking across the water at Manhattan."

"Is the treasure there?"

"I think so, Jack."

"Then where's X marks the spot? Isn't that what treasure maps show?"

"That's only in stories," snaps Kiko.

"But there's a story here," I say, tapping the bottom left. "Look. Pictures. There's a drawing of a ship."

"A sloop or a schooner," says Jack. "Built for speed."

"Maybe a pirate ship?"

"Or a clipper ship. Merchants wanted to move goods fast."

"Maybe," I muse. "Strange, the compass only aims north. No markings for south, east, or west. Nautical compasses would have all windward directions."

"And this is the harbor," I add. "See the dock, buildings. Stick figures."

"A man, woman, and child holding hands," exclaims Kiko. "You can tell by their sizes."

Quiet, we lie on our stomachs, studying the mysterious images. Hip-Hop sniffs the paper.

"Is this supposed to be a road?"

"Some lines are solid. Others are parallel dashes," says Kiko.

"Like train tracks," argues Jack.

"Leading to this settlement of tiny houses," I say. "And, beyond, a dozen teeny-tiny graveyard crosses."

"So weird." Jack shakes his head. "The city never had trains chugging through its center."

"A cemetery doesn't fit either." I sigh.

"That's right," answers Jack. "Dead don't need treasure."

Hip-Hop's nose keeps lifting the map's edge.

"Okay, okay," I say, turning the map over.

I whistle, amazed.

Railroad Agent, the North Star

is inscribed, boldly, mysteriously, at the bottom.

"Who's the agent? What? Who's 'North Star'? Why isn't there a name?"

"What's this?" Jack points at numbered prose. Three columns in total stretch across the map's back.

I read aloud:

One: Set sail. Gold is black; black is gold. Red is always red.
  Port City landing. A wooden wall becomes a market.

"It's a clue," Kiko shouts excitedly.

Hip-Hop barks, wagging his entire body.

I touch the yellowing map. "Three columns. Three clues?"

Kiko reads:

  Two: Oyster man, scoop from sand. Eat.
Pirates raid the black pearls. Stow the shells, stow the meat.
  Beware. Two-headed snake.

"Here it says 'Three,' but underneath, it's blank," I say. "The handwriting is different, too."

"So is the ink. Clues one and two, I think, were written with calligraphy ink. It's similar to *sumi*, which my dad uses. Three is a numeral, more modern, drawn in ballpoint."

"Doesn't make any sense," complains Jack. "Why have two clues, then nothing written for the third?"

"I don't know," I say, breathless. "But Kiko's right. The different ink and handwriting suggests the map changed hands. Maybe it was stolen?"

"Or hidden," insists Kiko.

"Ages ago. Then found but—"

"Hidden again?" Jack asks, astounded.

"Yes. How many years passed before Captain Maddie found the map? A hundred? Then she hid it again. It's a puzzle."

"Whoa," Jack cries. "Unbelievable. How could someone not need the treasure?"

"Ssssh!" I look up. One of the curtains fluttered. Probably the nosy reverend. I hear Ma calling, "Zane. Are you kids all right?"

"Fine."

"Just super," hollers Jack. "We're good, Mrs. Williams."

"They'll come tonight," whispers Kiko.

"Who?"

"Rattler. The kid who made fun of me at the skate

park. He'll bring others and terrorize the house. We have to defend it."

"Tell the police," pipes Kiko.

"They won't believe us," I say. "They'll just think we're lying."

"Yeah, I get it. My dad accuses me of lying all the time."

Kiko and I glance at each other.

"I've got to protect Ma," I say.

"And the map, too," argues Kiko. "A treasure would help you both. It's different than finding money in the captain's room."

"Money?" Jack's brows raise.

"Yeah. Mrs. Williams only took what was owed her."

"That was—"

"Don't say it." I glare at Jack. He was going to say "stupid." I get it—Jack's dad never gives him money. Instead, he buys alcohol. When he leaves for trucking trips, he never tells Jack and his mother when he's coming back, never leaves enough money for food and bills.

"This is different," says Kiko. "Captain wanted you to have her cane. Have this map. She called you first mate and wanted you to have the treasure."

"If we find the treasure, we'll split it. Three ways."

"That's what I'm talking about." Jack grins.

"We've got to solve the clues one by one," I say, determined.

Kiko flips the map.

We three stare at the island, the ship sailing north, an island with odd tracks, and the silhouette of a family holding hands.

"This map is real. I know it. It's trying to tell us something important. Else Rattler wouldn't have left the black spot."

"What spot?" asks Kiko.

I reach in my pocket, pulling out the folded white square. I open it.

"Super weird," says Jack. "Dead black. Looks like an eclipse."

"It's a threat." I slap the paper down. "Rattler doesn't know Captain Maddie is dead. He'll try to steal the map again."

"We'll keep it safe." Kiko starts rolling the map to fit inside the hollow cane.

I stroke Hip-Hop, thinking how hard Captain Maddie fought. How she made me first mate.

"You didn't ask for this, Zane," says Kiko.

"I woke up wanting an adventure. Hip-Hop did, too."

He licks my nose.

"What would a first mate do?" I murmur, staring into Hip-Hop's soulful eyes. "Fight. Follow the map."

Jack leaps up, bouncing on his toes, throwing punches. "We'll show Rattler and anyone else. A show of force. Right, Zane?" *Pop-pop.* "On our boards, we'll protect the house. Kiko, get your bamboo sword. You'll smack them if they make a move."

"I'll bring helmets, too."

"Aw, Kiko. Give me a break."

"Skate safe."

"Blah, blah, blah," teases Jack.

He smirks; Kiko scolds. Both enjoy the bickering.

Smiling, I twist the snake-heads handle back onto the cane. It feels right—the three of us together, Jack and Kiko squabbling like siblings; me, the responsible older brother. Finding treasure would help Ma. But first things first: I promised to "be the man of the house." Protecting our home comes first. "Home ownership is freedom," Dad used to say.

I stand, scan the streets, the neighborhood. We don't have a fence. Rattler and his crew can cut across the grass or walk right up the driveway.

On the horizon, far out into the Atlantic, clouds gather. Maybe there's an incoming storm?

I imagine Captain Maddie, alive, sailing through a hurricane. She would've loved it.

Would I?

Will I?

Rattler gave Captain Maddie the black spot. Did someone give the spot to Rattler?

Someone worse?

Unsettled, I hold up the black spot; it blocks the sun on the horizon. To my right, I think I see a shift, an afterimage. *Captain Maddie?*

Why has the map been lost, then found, lost, then found again?

Why has it come to me?

3

Night Attack

Me, Jack, and Kiko execute our plan. All afternoon, Jack carries buckets of sand from the beach, spreading it on the driveway and sidewalk. "They won't be able to skate on that," he crows.

Kiko's in charge of lanterns and flashlights. At night, Rockaway neighborhoods get super dark. Only the boardwalk glows with streetlamps, neon, and flashing lights.

I beg the arcade attendant for a bag of baseballs. Despite their twisting heads, I'm expert at aiming balls inside the Laughing Clowns' hollow mouths.

The three of us marvel at our handiwork. For extra protection, Kiko's brought her *shinai*, a bamboo practice sword.

Hip-Hop's my ace. Small but fierce.

Jack pets Hip-Hop, asking, like always, "Killed any rats today?"

We wait. The air becomes misty, cooler. The sun

burns orange-red, lowering deep beyond the horizon. In the distance, the boardwalk sparkles.

Jack's bruising for a fight. His hands clench, unclench.

Kiko's still as a statue. Collecting, channeling energy. "It's the Shinto way," she says when she lets me watch her train.

My stomach is in knots. My mind echoes, "Black is gold. Gold is black." Captain wanted me to find the treasure.

I've got to find the treasure.

Hip-Hop whimpers. I crouch beside him. "He smells them," I whisper. "Quiet." We're all statues now. Even Hip-Hop.

It's near midnight; the house and porch lights are off. On the empty street, shadows sail in slow motion. Six skaters dressed in black, canvassing the house. White hair glints. Rattler!

"Fire!" I cry.

Kiko flips the switch, and lanterns flame bright, lighting the yard. Hip-Hop dives, racing across the grass, and bites someone. A scream. Jack is right behind Hip-Hop, punching right, left. Shouting, "Come on, come on."

Some try. Kicking the pavement, then tumbling, their boards and wheels stuck, clogged with sand.

I throw the baseballs. Another scream. *Hit*—a

shoulder. *Hit*—a stomach. *Hit, hit, hit*—I'm rapid firing.

Kiko, gripping two flashlights in each hand, waves the beams, catching startled, contorted faces. All boys. Bigger, older than me.

I whistle. Hip-Hop runs back to me.

Rattler yells, "You'll pay for this. Tell Captain Maddie the treasure is ours."

"Get out of here," I holler, throwing a flurry of balls at Rattler. Kiko and Jack throw, too. Some boys try blocking with their skateboards. Others limp away. Another runs, spinning his wheels, shaking out sand.

Retreating, Rattler skates off smooth, quick. Outpacing his crew.

Grinning, me and Jack high-five, celebrate.

As if on cue, the reverend, his head poking out the second-story window, screeches, "Will you kids be quiet?" All the bedroom windows light up. Exasperated, her hair in curlers, Ma exclaims, "Zane!"

"Sorry, Ma," I say, suppressing my glee.

"Yeah. Sorry," echoes Jack, playfully punching my arm.

"So, so sorry," Kiko chimes with the biggest smile.

On the porch, we keep our mouths shut until, one by one, each bedroom light clicks off.

Nighttime silence again. No fighting or hollering, just normal sounds of waves hitting the shore and breezes rustling branches, leaves.

"Pirates," says Kiko.

We all saw the skull and bones bright, glowing on the topside of their skateboards.

"They don't know the captain is dead," I murmur.

"Meaning?' asks Jack.

I grip the porch rail. "Once they know, they'll come for me. Us."

Quiet, side by side, like on a ship's deck, we stand beneath stars, staring into darkness.

4

Sailing to Manhattan

Me, Jack, and Kiko stand on the wharf, waiting for the ferry. We all have our backpacks, our skateboards, and helmets. We've brought flashlights, snack bars, and water bottles. We're ready.

"Did you leave notes for your folks?" asks Kiko.

"Left Ma a letter. Told her I was searching for treasure." My heart quickens. "She'll be mad."

"You, Jack?"

He ignores Kiko, staring across the lapping waves. "I've never been on a ferry. Never been to Manhattan."

"Me neither," I add.

Kiko stares at her feet.

"Oh, but *you* have," I tease.

Kiko shoves me.

"Rich girl," snarks Jack.

"Don't gang up on me." Kiko's not angry. But she shoves Jack off-balance. "Mom and Dad take me to

Broadway shows, sightseeing, Central Park, the Shinto Foundation. The city's amazing."

"You'll guide us. Be our navigator."

"If we knew where we were going," grumbles Jack.

"I've got maps," says Kiko, defensive. "From the internet."

"You did good, Kiko." I smile. Kiko always overprepares. If the world was ending, she'd be the likeliest to survive.

"But Jack's right. We need the treasure map to tell us where to go." I reach back, touching the cane sticking out of my backpack. The snake heads are hidden, buried in the bottom.

"Kiko can navigate what's real. Captain Maddie's map is a puzzle."

The ferry's horn blasts. Again. And again.

"It's coming to port," I shout.

The ferry's a sleek blue-and-white two-level ship. On the open-air top, people sit, facing away from the New York skyline, eating donuts, sipping coffee, and raising their faces toward the sun. It's exciting seeing the ferry glide, parting water and making waves. It slows, nearing the wharf. Crew jump and rope the ship to the wharf's anchors.

The engine quiets.

American and New York flags fly, rippling high above

the stern. It's thrilling. I blink, imagining Captain Maddie, hands on her hips, standing beneath a pirate flag. She'd be happy, in command of everything she saw.

"I'm glad you're both with me."

Jack slaps my back; Kiko inches closer. We're a team.

Topside, dozens of happy people walk down the plank.

It's wondrous watching folks mingle, welcome one another, or dash onto land toward the boardwalk. Carrying coolers, heading to the beach.

I turn, scanning the crowds for Rattler.

"Hip-Hop!" shouts Kiko.

He's running, zigzagging down the wharf between cars, people.

"He's going to get himself killed," I yell.

"Hip-Hop." I run toward him. He leaps into my arms. "Bad boy." He licks my face; his tail wags.

Jack tousles his fur. "Hey, how goes it, rat dog?"

"He can't come," I blurt.

"Why not?" asks Jack.

"Pets aren't allowed on the ferry."

"Hip-Hop's not a pet. He's another navigator. He'll sniff out treasure."

"What're you doing?"

Jack's stooping, unloading his backpack, including his board. "Kiko, carry my stuff. I'll hold my board." He lifts the hood.

"Hop, Hip-Hop."

And Hip-Hop does. Jack closes the backpack top. Not too tight. Room enough for air. Eyes to peek.

I shake my head, slap Jack's back. He knows I don't like to be without Hip-Hop.

"No problem," says Jack, then, more seriously, "Friends."

"Best friends," I say.

"Shipmates," Kiko chuckles. "We're sailing for treasure."

Hip-Hop whines.

"Stop complaining," I say.

Jack slips his arms under the backpack straps, adjusts the waist clasp. "Row, row, row your boat . . ." He strides up the ramp. Me and Kiko follow.

On board, Jack ducks into a passageway and climbs the stairs. The upper-deck seats are mostly empty. Hardly anyone returning to Manhattan. Feels like a ghost ship.

I catch my breath, worrying if we made a mistake.

The ferry gives four blasts.

"We're leaving port," shouts Kiko. "The captain's warning the other boats."

The engine revs. With a click and churn, the ship lurches, then smooth, floats across the water.

The deck feels loose, like a huge skateboard beneath my feet.

"Make way, make way," heralds Jack, his hand waving away the smaller boats.

"Set sail," I yell.

"This is great," Jack whoops, his hand tamping down his blowing hair.

"An adventure." Kiko claps.

From the backpack, Hip-Hop snorts, juts out his head.

Crisp, breezy air, the engine humming, the hull breaking through waves, seagulls screeching above— all of it, awesome.

We're shipmates, sailing. We cheer.

Hip-Hop howls. I don't have the heart to say "hush." I take him out of the backpack and hold him. No one's going to throw him overboard. It's too late. We're sailing Jamaica Bay.

Wall Street

"**A**re we there yet?"
Kiko groans.

"Are we? Are we there yet?"

"Stop it, Jack."

"What? Stop, what? What? What? Are we there yet?" Jack cracks up. He loves being annoying.

Kiko groans again. "It's a short ride to Wall Street station!"

The ferry took us to Pier 11, Manhattan. Now we're on a subway.

Standing, Jack peers at the laminated subway map. "Heh, Kiko, we could've walked from the ferry. Or skated. It would've been faster."

Sheepish, Kiko hunches in her seat. "I like subways," she mutters.

"Are you kidding me?" Jack smacks his palm to his forehead.

"Cool it, Jack. Kiko's allowed to like subways."

Jack grumbles.

Kiko stuffs her hands into her pockets.

A ferry. Now a subway ride. I like all of it. Like me and Kiko (Hip-Hop happy in the backpack) lurching against one another as the car sways.

Twirling, staggering for fun, Jack grips the steel pole.

Dozens of people are on the subway. Some get on, get off. A flurry of colors; pastel dresses; rough, blue denim, coming and going. Men, women, the occasional kid. Normal folk.

They ignore us.

Except one.

I look at the kid in the back of the car. Short, skinny, he's slouching against a pole. Black sweatpants and black T-shirt. He's wearing silver reflective sunglasses and a blue bandanna tied around his neck. The bandanna throws me. Used to seeing bandannas on people's heads, not around their throats.

I stare.

He turns away, ducks behind a man wearing shorts.

I'm sure I saw him on the ferry, too, when we disembarked. (Is he following us?)

Kiko watches me. She always seems to know when I'm worrying.

I murmur, "Just tired, Kiko."

"Hungry, too," complains Jack.

"Eat one of your snack bars," snaps Kiko.

"I don't have any."

"Take one of mine."

Eager, Jack digs into my backpack.

The subway hisses, rattles on the rails, a recorded voice announces stops, warns "Don't lean against the subway doors." More riders get on than off. Now the car is crowded. I can't see the kid. Only flashes of the blue bandanna, shifting left, right. It disappears.

Before he loses a seat, Jack sits next to me. "Why're we going to Wall Street anyway?"

"Again, Jack?" Kiko rolls her eyes.

Keeping my voice low, I say, "It's a feeling."

"Intuition," adds Kiko.

Jack snaps, "Smarty pants."

Kiko sticks out her tongue.

"Stop it. Both of you. Hip-Hop's more mature than either of you."

Hip-Hop pokes his head up.

"'Set sail.' We've done that. 'Gold is black; black is gold. Red is always red.' I don't know what that means. But the gold's got to mean wealth. 'Port City landing.' Lower Manhattan.

"See," says Kiko, unfolding a map on her lap. "Nothing but ports. Ships sail in and out into the harbor.

Cruise ships, merchant ships, yachts, sailing ships—you name it. All of them coming from across the ocean." She circles the harbor with a red marker. "Want to hear a weird fact?"

"No," says Jack as I sigh. We both know we're going to hear it anyway.

"September 11. Yes! Another one. September 11, 1609. Henry Hudson sailed into New York Bay. The Dutch first settled New York, called it 'New Amsterdam.'"

"Who cares?" asks Jack.

"I get it," I say. "Lower Manhattan is where the city started. First colony. First port. First economy. Almost four hundred years later, terrorists attack. The World Trade Center is only two-tenths of a mile from Wall Street."

"Wall Street," chortles Jack. "Follow the money."

"Yes! We're headed in the right direction. To capitalism's heart, past and present. Port, ships, trading, gold, financial district. This has to be where we solve the first clue."

The three of us smile. Kiko giggles happily. Jack laughs.

The subway squeals.

"Our stop," Kiko exclaims, standing up.

"I've got Hip-Hop." Jack stands, grabs his backpack. "Killed any rats today?"

I slip my backpack onto my shoulders. Steady myself as the car jerks to a stop and the doors slide open.

Wall Street Station

People are trying to get in while we're trying to get out.

I look right. A subway door down, I see the blue bandanna. My reflection in the sunglass mirrors.

Shoving past people, the kid (smaller than me) exits the car.

On the platform, I search for him. Mass of moving people. Loud, shrill noises as the subway moves again.

"What's the matter, Zane?" asks Kiko.

"What?"

"You're not moving," snaps Jack.

I frown. "I thought I saw someone."

"Sure, you did. There're people everywhere," Kiko says logically.

"Paranoid?" Jack asks.

"No." I'm anxious, worried. Rattler is still hunting us. I'm not imagining it. It's for real. "We're being followed."

"Like I said, paranoid."

We take the stairs, surfacing like moles from underground darkness into open-air sunlight.

I've never seen so many buildings, crowded streets, rushing people. It's a wild, noisier world apart from Rockaway.

Looking over my shoulder, I scan for spies.

"What must this have looked like hundreds of years ago?" asks Kiko.

I blink.

Color drains. The world is sepia—reddish brown like an old photograph. Men on horseback, fancy carriages on dirt-packed streets.

Two- and four-story brick buildings. Gentlemen and clerks walk purposefully. Rich ladies carry parasols. Merchants bow. White people buy and sell. Black and brown people carry packages, rein horses. Others, white but poorer, push carts. Chestnuts, pretzels for sale.

I blink again.

"The past is never past," I hear.

"Captain Maddie?" I turn, searching for a ghost.

I shake myself, clearing my head, telling myself not to go crazy. Focus on the here, now.

It's late afternoon. Skyscrapers and thick buildings block sunlight.

Town cars, taxis, and delivery trucks jam the streets. People walk briskly down sidewalks—some jaywalking between cars, others moving in and out of offices, between columns of granite or marble. Tourists peer at brochures, chatter, and point.

Jack gawks. "Look at New York now." He puts down

his board and sails, zigzagging down the road. He yells, joyous, "Yahoo," zooming faster and faster, steering between cars (a taxi honks!) and, leaping up and down, over the sidewalk, startling people. Hip-Hop's barking wildly, enjoying every roll.

"That's Jack." I shrug, then set sail, following him.

"Stop!" Kiko laughs. "Stop, stop. You're going the wrong way!"

Me and Jack spin, doubling back toward Kiko. There's no clear path. Even the bicycle lane is blocked— sanitation workers loading trash, a yellow food truck advertising burgers and breakfast burritos.

We pause at the street corner. Across from Wall Street station, I see an odd stranger. Glimpse old-fashioned bell-bottom pants.

A man with locs, strands of gold necklaces, and braided bands around his wrists, stands on the sidewalk, his back and one foot propped against a building. His shirt is bright red, and his pants are black bell-bottoms with wide white stripes down the sides. Most folks are in dark suits carrying briefcases and computer bags. This guy reminds me of Dad when he once dressed like a hippie for Halloween. Or Caesar, the carny barker, who, during summers, rules Rockaway's boardwalk.

He nods at me.

Not sure why, I nod back.

"Down Broadway," says Kiko, kicking hard for more speed. "Follow me."

"To adventure!" I holler.

Skating, the wind parting about me, feels as good as the ferry ride.

"Ahoy," I yell, sounding like a first mate. Hip-Hop and Jack sail with me, our bodies leaning into the wind, avoiding potholes, cars, people. Even a cop on a horse.

We follow Kiko, our navigator.

"Stop."

Jack does a slide full stop. I'm envious of how Jack's so abrupt yet smooth. I slow gradually. Hip-Hop sits and waits for me to stop.

Kiko's talking. "This is Trinity Church. The internet says it's the oldest, most famous church in New York. Built in 1697."

"Took forever," says Jack.

"They didn't have cranes, backhoes, or bulldozers," I say.

"It's Gothic Revival architecture," Kiko says.

"What's that mean?"

"Look at it!" snaps Kiko, exasperated.

Red-brown brick, the church is beautiful. Elaborate spires edge the buildings. The highest spire reaches toward heaven with a stained-glass front showing Jesus and the saints. Higher, there's a bell chamber and a clock tower. Below, a huge bronze door to enter the church.

"It's beautiful," I say.

"Look here." We follow her around the side of the church, a small cemetery with headstones, crosses, and a large granite tomb.

Kiko throws her hands up and outward. "'I am not throwing away my shot,'" she belts like she's onstage.

"What're you singing about?"

"Alexander Hamilton. *Hamilton*, the musical. This is Alexander's grave. He was the first secretary of the US Treasury. Wall Street's beginning."

"Cool," says Jack. "Wall Street, where money gets made."

Kiko keeps prattling. "Tons of famous financial buildings here—the Federal Reserve, NY Stock Exchange, the J.P. Morgan Building."

Jack's listening avidly.

I'm half listening. Hip-Hop's ears are up.

I swallow, swearing I hear the whirl of skateboard wheels. A special *whoosh, whizzing.*

"If treasure's anywhere, it'd be here. Wall Street, hoot, hoot!" Jack's jumping, wailing. "Money land."

Holding Hip-Hop's front paws, Kiko sways, humming "My Shot."

I scan the street, the wide Broadway and Wall Street

intersection. Wheels sounding louder. I backtrack toward the church door. Nothing unusual. But the *whizzing* grows louder. No creaks, squeaks, just a steady drone of hard, expensive wheels. Pro wheels, not amateurs.

"Get out the map," says Jack, slapping my back, startling me. He lifts the cane out of my backpack.

"Give it back!" I yell.

"What's the matter with you?" asks Kiko, standing on the church steps.

"It isn't safe."

"If treasure's going to be anywhere, it'll be here," argues Jack.

A clump of Hip-Hop's fur rises.

The *whiz-whizzing* is shriller.

"It's a trap."

"What?" squawks Kiko.

Hip-Hop growls, barks.

Boards appear from alleys, around street corners. Some even dive from behind marble columns into the streets. Every which way, a silent crew is zooming down Broadway's street and sidewalks. Folks yell; some are knocked down. Horns honk. Some drivers, getting out of their cars, curse at the skaters. A policeman on a bike, unable to stop them, skids into the bushes.

It's a swarm. No, more like a wave. The skaters weave among traffic, but come closer, ever closer together, unifying in motion, like a ship barreling toward Trinity Church. There's no denying they're coming straight at us, relentless. Black-clothed, pirate wild.

"Jack!" I scream.

He throws Kiko the cane and comes to stand beside me. "Distract," he says.

I nod, gazing out from the church steps.

People scurry away. Food cart vendors retreat. Folks sense a struggle is about to go down. The sidewalk clears. The *whizzing*, rumbling wheels are overwhelming.

As the skaters close in on us, traffic swerves, inches forward.

Brave, ready for a fight, Jack sails into the gang, his board sideswiping other boards, his hands shoving, unbalancing the skaters.

"Keep the cane safe, Kiko."

Kiko's in warrior stance—knees slightly bent, weight centered. Eyes focused forward, she walks backward toward the church door.

Unexpectedly, two skaters dash out from each side of the church. Kiko flings the cane outward, hitting one boy's leg.

"Oww," he screams.

Roaring, I dart and chase the second kid. "Yeah, you better run." Then I turn toward the limping skater, clutching his board. He lurches, rolls awkwardly down the steps.

"Hide, Kiko. Keep the cane safe."

Jack is thrashing, fighting.

A kid pulls Jack's arms behind his back. I leap, skate down the stairs, hard stop, then pull the kid off Jack while Jack punches back at three kids trying to get a hit.

Hip-Hop hops on a board, biting a kid's ankles. He leaps off as the kid spins, retreating.

Off our boards, me and Jack are dead in the water. Skaters, like sharks, taunt, zigzagging on black boards, looking for weaknesses. Me and Jack are back-to-back, fending off punches.

The kid with mirrored sunglasses and a blue bandanna hits me hard.

Breathless, I double over.

The other skaters stop, forming a line. One foot on their boards; the other on the ground, ready to kick.

I see the bandanna kid look back and upward. I follow his gaze.

Rattler—sauntering down a building's concrete steps.

He's taller than I remembered. His hair is still shockingly silvery-white.

"Red Flag," he shouts, makes a fist, then twists his hand and thumb down.

"Arrrgh," they scream, rushing in, shoving, kicking, beating us.

Jack gets pinned, his face pressing against asphalt. I tug one kid off before I'm pounded in the gut and taken down.

My sight is blurred by a flurry of sneakers and Hip-Hop growling, snapping at legs.

I curl into a ball, clasp my head.

Angrily, Jack shrieks, lifts his body, throwing, pulling tormentors off his back. He's in "Hulk mode." He's protecting me, taking all the heat, the hard hits.

Grunting, I clamber up. Back-to-back, me and Jack give as good as we can.

"Make way!"

The skate crew parts, making space for Rattler. He skates slow. Stops. The blue-bandanna kid stands beside him.

From the west, another kid sails up, dangling our backpacks.

Jack reaches. "Give them back."

The blue-bandanna kid shoves him.

Off-balance, Jack falls.

"Good work, Petey," says Rattler. The kid smiles like he's won a prize. Next to Rattler and the other boys, he seems young. Almost a mascot. He's fierce, punches above his weight.

I stoop to help Jack.

Rattler stoops, too, one hand on the ground, the other holding his board. Smirking, the bandage on his cheek wrinkles.

Sore, breathing heavily, I keep my eyes on Rattler. Though he didn't hit us, I know he's the real enemy.

"Stay down. Stay below," Rattler warns. "It suits you. Both of you." His eyes flicker. "Captain Maddie's dead, isn't she?"

I say nothing.

"We'll keep your backpacks. Maybe there's hidden treasure?" he jeers.

"A fair fight," Jack spits. "Let's have a fair fight."

"A first mate gives orders. The crew does the dirty work."

The kids behind and beside Rattler laugh.

Rattler stands, hand signals "Let's go!"

Every board starts rolling. Cruising in unison. Impressive. A crew moving, seemingly connected, as naturally as a snake's skin.

Traffic starts moving again. Folks walk, some checking their cell phones, some bobbing their heads to earbud music.

Hip-Hop's still chasing the skaters. I whistle. He stops, turns, his head tilted, questioning me.

"C'mon, Hip-Hop," I shout. He runs, leaping into my arms. He licks my face, leans over and licks Jack, too.

I scan the street. Back to normal, like nothing happened.

"Payback, Zane. I'm ready for payback."

Bloodred bruises cover his face and arms. More, I know, are hidden beneath his shirt. He took the brunt of the beating. He hates to see me or anyone bullied. "You okay?"

"I'm okay." He smiles ruefully. "My dad hits worse."

I guide Jack back to the sidewalk.

Hip-Hop snarls, barks ferociously.

I look up.

Honking, yelling, "Get out the way. Get out the way."

Rattler. Standing in the middle of the road. Town cars and taxis swerve to avoid hitting him.

Holding his sleek black board across his body, he looks sinister.

I stand tall.

A face-off.

Rattler flips his board. The white graphic is clear. A skull. Crossbones.

"Ahoy," he calls, then hops onto his board, right leg kicking, and rides toward the ocean, the afternoon sun.

Score: One to Nothing

Defeated, me, Jack, and Hip-Hop retreat to the church steps. Our backpacks, helmets, IDs, phones, and wallets are gone. Only our boards are safe. And the map.

On cue, Kiko peeks out the church door. "Over?"

"Yeah," I say, grateful she's got her backpack and, most importantly, Captain Maddie's cane.

"You two took a beating."

Jack flushes red. "Payback. I'm going to beat down every single one of them."

"Violence won't solve anything."

"Kiko's right. Finding the treasure, not revenge— that's what it's all about."

Sullen, Jack says, "I'm tired of being beat." Shoulders slumped, he massages his side.

Me and Kiko exchange glances.

"Jack, you were right to bring Hip-Hop. Did you

see him grab that kid? Leaped right to his butt. He's a fighter."

Jack opens his arms.

Hip-Hop dashes, puts his paws on Jack's chest. "Good boy. You killed them rats today!" He scratches Hip-Hop's ears. "Their boards were rocking. Got to admit that. Zane, did you see Rattler's board? Slick. Must've cost a fortune."

"He's still a jerk," responds Kiko.

"He wanted what we have." I pace up and down the steps.

Kiko, Jack, and Hip-Hop stare. No one says anything.

"If the captain's dead, we're on the move. . . ."

"We're hunting for treasure," adds Jack.

And Rattler's hunting us, I think but don't say.

I stop pacing. "'Set sail.'"

"We did that," answers Kiko.

"'Gold is black; black is gold. Red is always red.'"

"Money's green," says Jack. "Don't get 'black.'"

"Gold is green. I mean, money," adds Kiko. "Gold bars. Gold coins in the Treasury."

"Treasury? Treasure?" muses Jack.

I stop pacing. "'Red is always red.' I don't get it." I sit on the step above them. "What if Wall Street was Port City landing?"

"That makes sense," says Kiko. "Lower Manhattan was a major port even in the 1600s."

"So?" asks Jack. "Everybody from back then is dead."

Kiko sticks out her tongue.

"Who cares about history? Only now is real."

"Not true, Jack," I say, touching the canc. "The map proves it's not so. Else we wouldn't be searching for treasure."

Jack shrugs.

"'A wooden wall becomes a market.' That's concrete, real," I say. "The connection's here. Got to be. 'Wall' as in—"

"Wall Street," pipes Kiko.

"'Market' as in stock market. But there wouldn't have been stocks back then. Something else. Something valuable."

I look outward. Everyone seems rich. In nice clothes, carrying laptops and Starbucks cups. Even the food carts are doing good business. Lots of Rockaway folks struggle. Especially during winter. The Boardwalk drifters panhandle. Tourist trinkets don't sell. Pretzels, popcorn, and cotton candy become stale.

I swallow hard. "Ma's fighting to keep our home. We might lose it."

"Oh no," cries Kiko.

"I've got to find the treasure. We need it."

"Fan out."

"That's it, Jack. We'll cover more ground," I shout eagerly. "Sure to find something." Jack and I high-five.

He raises his brows at Kiko.

"Okay, okay, okay," she grumbles. "You're smart when you want to be."

Jack laughs.

"Kiko, you keep the cane. Seriously. Jack and I are still hurting. I trust you."

"Thanks, Zane."

We three stand.

"Hip-Hop comes with me."

On the pavement, we lay down our boards. Look at each other.

Kiko's intense. Jack isn't angry but relaxed, arms swinging.

I nod. "Thanks."

"Don't say it," quips Jack.

"Friends don't need to say it," adds Kiko.

"I'll go south."

"West."

"East for me, then," hoots Jack. "Set sail."

"Again," shouts Kiko.

"Set sail," we all shout.

"Sunset," I say. "Meet back here. At Trinity."

Kiko nods.

"Sail!" insists Jack.

We set sail, wheels *whizzing*, rolling our boards in different directions through the congested roads and streets.

Hip-Hop growls. I look to where he's looking.

For the second time, I see the bell-bottom man—
hands on hips, feet firmly planted, staring at me
Like he knows me. Or wants to know me.
Why?

Discovery

I skate in a grid—down one block, looking to the right, then turn and skate back up the block, looking to the left. Block by block by block. It's hard searching for what I don't know, avoiding traffic, people opening taxi doors, jaywalkers, even dogwalkers. My board isn't the best. But I swerve in and out. Hip-Hop, by my side, gives me a wider berth.

My neck itches. Someone's watching me. Another spy?

I kick my board up. Stop. Look this way and that. Solid gray, black, brown, and navy suits; gray stone buildings, black town cars, asphalt streets, light gray concrete. The only bright color is yellow—honking taxis. From the corner of my eye, a flash of wide white stripes—red and black. But it must be a mirage—as soon as I turn my head—nothing. No crew in black. No one.

I continue my grid search, turning the corner to a

new block. Water Street. Up, then turn around, skating north. Block after block. Impossible. Stupid idea.

Never any treasure. Just a crazy captain.

A tourist is aiming a camera at a green sign in front of a Verizon store. Weird. Who takes photos of signs?

I skate up.

The woman murmurs, "It's really a shame." Shaking her head, she walks away.

I look closer at the sign. The lettering is white. There's an illustration of an old town built by the water with partial sketches of two sailing ships. You can't tell whether they're arriving or departing.

NEW YORK'S MUNICIPAL SLAVE MARKET

Whoa. What?

Slavery was introduced to Manhattan in 1626. By the mid-eighteenth century, approximately one in five people living in New York City was enslaved and almost half of Manhattan households included at least one slave.

Unbelievable. Slaves in the North? New York?

I feel sick.

"Cruel, isn't it?"

I spin around. It's the bell-bottom man. Hip-Hop growls.

"Hush."

"Dogs like me." His smile is electric, warming. He pulls out something brown from his pocket. Jerky?

I worry about strangers giving Hip-Hop food, but before I can say anything, Hip-Hop growls again.

"Stop it, Hip-Hop."

Bowing, the man sweeps off a pretend hat. He's tall with large, light brown eyes. He reminds me of the carny barkers during Rockaway summers. Broad shoulders, huge smile, hands constantly in motion. Bigger than life.

He peers down at Hip-Hop. "He'll get used to me." Then, "What happened to your face? Who hurt you?"

"This skateboard crew." My voice chokes; I'm embarrassed by the beating.

As if he'd read my thoughts, he asks, "Did anybody help you?"

I shake my head. Dad helped everybody. Everyone in the neighborhood loved him.

He touches my shoulder. "I'm sorry."

Strange. I feel almost like crying. Dad used to touch my shoulder gently, encouragingly.

He taps his finger on the sign. "Disgrace it took so long for New York to acknowledge its slave past. Before Wall Street was Wall Street, it was a marketplace. For people.

"They built a wall, did you know? Built a wall to sell men, women, children brought as cargo off ships."

"A wall?" I stare at the painted letters. So freaky; these marks are talking about people. In my mind, I see the treasure map, its black ink drawings of men, women, and children.

"The wall was here, didn't you know?"

"What?"

"On this street," he murmurs, draping his arm about my shoulder. "Between Water and Pearl. Look," he says, his other arm sweeping through air, encompassing the roads paralleling the East River, the outlet to the bay, and the port.

I shiver.

"Look! Good people captured, starved, sickened on ships. Coming to the New World. Not just Virginia, mind you. New York had lots of slaves. Over two million built this city. Made it the greatest city in the world. While they and their descendants got nothing. Nothing, mind you."

His voice is rolling with power. And I *see*. I really do. *Images flicker, come to life.*

Before, in my mind, images looked like photographs. Now they seem like a silent movie. (What's happening to me?)

Figures move, stumble. I see a long line of shackled people, some stumbling, some wailing, being brought to where I'm standing now.

"This was the place. A wall built for selling people. Advertising them. Corner of Wall Street and Water. Chained, locked to the wood like animals. Inspection, then auction."

I flatten my palm, covering the horrible words. A cheap sign. Painted green wood on stilts between two young, scrawny trees.

"You never learned this in school, did you now? Slave sales. Starting December 1711."

"They don't even show the people," I murmur. Just a picture of water, schooners, and buildings on shore. Looks like an old-time postcard.

"People's lives and spirits buried in words," he blusters. "Words painted in white, no less. They show ships as if the seamen were at fault. Sailors were just carrying trade. Merchants did the dirty work of funding trade, awarding, selling bounties."

"You sound like Captain—"

"Captain who? Who do I remind you of?" His head tilts, his eyes seeming to gaze deep inside me.

"No one," I say quickly, feeling on guard. I don't know why. He seems nice. But while his words sound like Captain Maddie's, his accent is strange. Jamaican like Raj, who runs the Ferris wheel, but Bronx, too, like Dave, who manages the carnival's ball-and-bucket toss.

Hands on his hips, he bellows, "I'm John. You've had a hard welcome to the city. Not as hard as slaves, mind you." He chuckles low. "Let me be a friend. Help you." He thrusts out his hand.

I almost shake it. His ring of silver twisting snakes stops me. (I'm confused.)

His expression is kind, sympathetic. Curious. (But Hip-Hop doesn't like him.)

"I've got to meet my friends at Trinity Church."

"Ah, that, too, was built by slaves."

"Really?"

"Yes, too bad, isn't it? A great treasure built by Black people, mind you. Look around now . . . everybody here mainly white, all wealthy.

"Mind you, back in time, on Stone Street's cobble-stones the whip lashed Black skin. Blood running red, being treated like gold."

Click-click: puzzle pieces fit inside my head.

The clue: Gold is black; black is gold. Red is always red.
Port City landing. A wooden wall becomes a market.
(I've got to tell Jack and Kiko.)

"Got to go."

"No, not yet," John exclaims, blocking my way.

I swerve around him. "Come on, Hip-Hop."

"I could teach you. History, Zane. I could teach you."

I keep speeding. Heart pounding, I hear John

shouting. I don't slow, turn around. Can't wait to tell my friends. There's a treasure after all. For real.

(How'd he know my name?)

Wind rushes over my face. I'm skating better than I've ever skated before. Veer left, veer right. Hop. *Snap.* Leap over the curb. Heading to Trinity. Sailing, top speed.

I blink. Crackling, black images float. Like wraiths. A soft breath, like a breeze, strokes my cheek.

Hip-Hop barks.

A taxi driver yells, "Get out the street. This ain't a park."

"Step on it, Hip-Hop." And we *zoom*, sailing, the wind at our backs.

Black Gold

We're in the church's vestibule with the map stretched between us.

"These stick figures are slaves. Wall Street used to be a market for slaves."

"Seriously?" asks Jack.

"Yeah. 'Gold is black; black is gold.'"

Kiko gasps. "The clue's about buying and selling people?"

"That's right, Kiko."

She types into her iPhone. "1625, the Dutch brought eleven African slaves to New Amsterdam."

"New Amsterdam?"

"That's what they called their colony, Jack. It was before New York was New York."

"What else?"

"By 1711—"

"Was it called New York then?"

"Yes," says Kiko. "Slaves were auctioned. Native Americans. Africans. Wow, oh, wow," she exclaims.

"What?"

"In 1800, one in five New Yorkers was a slave," she shrieks. "Half, *half* the people in Manhattan owned a slave."

"Slaves built this church," I say. "John told me."

"Who's John?" Kiko persists.

"A man I met," I say, ignoring Jack's gaze.

Kiko flushes with anger. "Disgusting. Slaves built the wall, the Wall Street *wall where they were sold.*"

She starts weeping, but she doesn't want us to see.

Jack touches the map's black schooner. "This represents slave ships coming to port." The bruise beneath his eye is turning blue-black. "'Everybody loves New York,'" he says, sarcastic.

"Hidden history, right?"

Jack nods.

"It matters." I turn the map over, my finger lingering on the words:

One: Set sail. Gold is black; black is gold. Red is always red.

"Red's got to be blood," I whisper.

Port City landing. A wooden wall becomes a market.

"The next column has the second clue."
Jack reads:

Two: Oyster man, scoop from sand. Eat.
Pirates raid the black pearls. Stow the shells, stow the meat.
Beware. Two-headed snake.

"That's what Captain Maddie told me. 'Beware the two-headed snake.'" I clutch the cane's handle, reminded of John's ring.

"If she had that cane, she must've been part of it," says Jack.

"What?"

"Betrayal."

"No," I answer. But I hear Maddie's voice, *I stole it.*

"What do you really know about her, Zane?" asks Kiko.

"What does anybody know about anybody?" mutters Jack.

"Captain Maddie was good." I can't explain how a black spot or any theft doesn't matter. I repeat emphatically, "She was good."

"Of course she was," soothes Kiko. "She liked you, Zane."

I feel guilty. I'm not telling them everything. Not how sad, moody she could be. How I reminded her of her son.

"Focus on the clue," urges Kiko. "What do oysters have to do with slavery?"

We're stumped.

"Maybe John knows?"

"Who's John?" Kiko persists.

"This stranger I met. Talked funny. But he knew history. Like you do, Kiko."

"I'm just internet surfing. Maybe this John guy can help?"

"But we won't tell him about the map," I warn.

"It's hard enough to split three ways."

Kiko shoves Jack. "What's that mean?"

"Nothing," mutters Jack.

"Equal shares," I insist. "Between us three."

Kiko and Jack are satisfied.

But I'm not. Captain Maddie trusted me. I trust Jack and Kiko. And, yet, I wonder if there's something more than maybe jewels, money, or gold? Some other secret?

Jack snores, his arm underneath his head on the marble floor. Kiko, half-awake, smacks him. Then she falls back asleep. Her backpack is her pillow.

Worrying, I can't fall asleep. What does a first mate do? A first mate steers the ship when the captain can't. But I don't know where I'm going, what I'm supposed to do.

I close my eyes. I *see* Captain Maddie.

*She's intent, watching me. Her head turns to some-
one I can't see. She nods, agreeing.*

To what? With whom?

I must be losing my mind. Yet everything I'm seeing,
hearing, even dreaming seems connected. Like Captain
Maddie is guiding me.

Opening my eyes, I pull the cane closer to me. I still
see the captain.

"I knew I could count on you, Zane."

(Inhale, exhale. Don't freak.)

Ears up, Hip-Hop sees and hears her, too.

She disappears.

I sigh. Hip-Hop sighs, snuggles against my chest. I
hold him close, feeling his heartbeat, his lungs expanding against my chest.

We'll hunt again tomorrow.

Oysters Are Better Than Apples

Sleeping in the vestibule cramped every bone in our bodies. Me and Jack (even Hip-Hop) are stiff, doubly sore from the fight. Only Kiko is rested, eager.

"Let's head to the library," she says outside, staring at her phone. "There's a public library named New Amsterdam. We're bound to find some answers to the second clue."

"Best to keep watch for those pirate skaters," says Jack.

Fearful, we look every which way. North, south, east, west. Up and down the streets.

I can't help looking for John, too. (Striped bell-bottoms are hard to miss.)

"Let's go," says Kiko, helmet on, skating off.

Me and Jack do our best to follow her, carefully weaving between people, food carts.

A woman shouts, "What a cute dog!" Some curse.

A man startles, drops his coffee cup. I yell, "Sorry," zooming by.

"This is it," says Kiko, stuffing her board next to the cane in her backpack, locking her helmet to its backstrap.

"This is what?" asks Jack. "It's an office building."

"The first floor is a branch library. Come on."

I shrug. "Yeah. Come on, Jack."

The library is bright, bustling with people. Kiko heads straight for a computer and types: Old New York. Oysters.

The screen fills with titles: *Encyclopedia of New York, Atlas of New York, A History of New York.*

"This one," exclaims Kiko. "*The Big Oyster.*"

"Don't get it," says Jack.

"Big Apple," I say excitedly. "Before New York was the Big Apple, it could've been the Big Oyster."

"That's right. *The Big Oyster: History on the Half Shell.* Down here." She moves through the maze of stacks. "There's a New York History section. Call number 973."

"The author?" I ask Kiko.

"Kurlansky. There. Grab it, Jack."

Jack, the tallest, pulls the book from the top shelf. He flips to the back cover.

"Oysters were the main crop of Native Americans,

settlers," I crow, "and . . . wait for it, wait for it . . . the
favorite food of early NEW YORKERS. High-five, Jack."

"Can I help you?" a round-faced woman with curly
hair asks Hip-Hop.

She's wearing jeans and a plaid shirt with buttons.
Lots and lots of buttons. Small and large, proclaiming:
"I Read Past My Bedtime." "Eat. Sleep. Read." Even a
purple button with a winged dragon: "Fantasy Reader."
And a black button with white lettering proclaiming:
"Straight Outta the Library."

I like her rainbow button best: "Just One More
Chapter."

"Dogs aren't allowed." She stoops, patting Hip-Hop's
head, coos, "Such a good boy."

Standing, she points to her shirt's collar. There's a
gold button with a dog's footprint.

"I love dogs." She sighs. "Still, he'll have
to leave."

"We need this book," I say.

"Do you have a library card? If not, you can apply
for one. But your dog has to go."

Hip-Hop stands on his hind legs, then sits, licks his
mouth, and stares upward with his puppy-dog eyes.

"He's a charmer. What's his name?"

"Hip-Hop."

"Cute. What're you kids looking for?"

"Books about early New York."

"You're in the right section. Look, here's my card. Come back without Hip-Hop. I'll help."

"Lorena Gutiérrez," I read.

"Flip it."

I do. There's a sketch of a dog.

"It's Leia. As in Princess. My two-year-old Jack Russell."

Giggling, Kiko bobs her head. "Maybe Hip-Hop's cousin?"

"Has she killed any rats?" asks Jack.

Startled, Ms. Gutiérrez answers, "Yes, yes, she has. My apartment building has plenty. Come on, now." Smiling, she escorts us to the door.

Still, people stare. Hip-Hop slinks. (Though he's done nothing wrong.)

We stumble into the sunshine. The library was cool, mellow, and dark.

"I'll go back in and apply for a card," I say.

"No need," says Jack, pulling a book from beneath his shirt.

"Jack." Kiko shoves him. "You stole it."

"Did not," he scolds, irritable. "Borrowed it."

"You've got to take it back, Jack."

"I will. After we're done with it. I promise. Look, there's maps, pictures of oystermen."

Kiko and I lean in.

"'Oyster man, scoop from the sand,'" I say, echoing the clue. "'Eat.'"

"Did someone say 'eat'?"

Startled, I look behind me. "John," I blurt.

"At your service." He bows, flourishing his hands. "Who're your charming friends?"

"I'm Kiko."

"Jack," says Jack.

"Oysters." John taps the book. "Best eaten raw. Or stewed. Hungry?"

We all groan. Except for sharing Kiko's remaining granola bars, we're starved.

"Come along. I'll show you real New York hospitality. Oysters, plump and tasty. Hot sauce, crackers. Did you know oysters are considered the food of love?"

Kiko rolls her eyes. Jack snickers. My stomach grumbles.

Ship Attack

We're on John's skiff, bouncing, riding over waves. Sails balloon with air. We're going oystering with John.

I thought we were going to a restaurant. I pat Hip-Hop's head. He's hungry, too.

John's steering the rudder.

Hip-Hop sniffs his butt. "Stop it, Hip-Hop," I say.

"No, he's a smart boy." John reaches into his back pocket. "Jerky. Just for you."

Hip-Hop twists his neck, looking at me.

"It's okay."

Hip-Hop takes the jerky gently from John's palm. He carries it to the stabilizing planks, where we stashed our skateboards and Kiko's backpack with the cane safe inside.

John smiles, pleased with himself.

(Who's John, really?) I ignore my uneasiness. We

need him to pilot. Oystering, I might understand the second clue.

Though I live on a beach, I've never dug for anything. Clams, mussels, oysters. They're easily bought at the grocery store. Or as takeout on the boardwalk.

But it feels terrific being outside, sailing with wind spraying water, mist on my face. I feel free, as good as if I'm sailing my skateboard. Kiko and Jack like it, too. We're happy, feeling the sun, smelling salt and algae. Forgetting about yesterday's fears.

"Can I try?"

John lets Jack hold the rudder and steer.

"Gently, boy. Keep it firm. Steer true. Keep the wind in our sails."

John claps, rubs his hands together. "Zane, check the rigging. Make sure it's tight."

Not sure what I'm doing, I touch the taut ropes. "It's fine," I yell. More than fine.

The billowing sail tilts the ship slightly on its edge. It feels like a skateboard rounding a tight corner on half its wheels.

"Jack and Zane, you remind me of midshipmen. In the olden days, boys as young as eight went to sea to learn how to be men."

"Sounds sexist."

"You're right, Miss Kiko. Still, the olden days held

lots of promise for boys who longed for adventure."
John gazes at me, slaps Jack on the back.

I'm amazed because Jack doesn't mind the hit
at all.

"What else about the olden days?" he asks.

"Olden days, good ole days, you could just dig up oysters from any place in New York Harbor. Dig them out
the sand." He mimes with his hands. "Crack and eat.

"Now they've got farms. So now we steal."

"Steal?" squeals Kiko.

"That's what oyster pirates do." John laughs, jovial.

"But we're not pirates," I say.

"Too bad. But for today, let's pretend you are."

Kiko glances at me, uneasy.

Jack is having a grand time. Even with a bruised,
busted-up face, he seems happier than I've seen him
in a long while.

"John? Is that your real name?" asks Jack.

"Call me whatever you like. John. Mike. Bill. We're
friends, are we not?"

Jack smiles wide.

"Swallow a sweet oyster," says John, "I bet you'll
forget your own name."

I say, "I think you'll hate it, Jack. An oyster is like
swallowing ocean Jell-O."

"Zane, you don't even like sushi," quips Kiko.

"How is it you've never had an oyster?" John asks Jack, retaking the rudder.

Jack stares at the boat's bottom. "My dad's a meat-and-potatoes man. So that's what we eat."

"Even when his dad isn't home," Kiko snaps, scowling.

Jack's face reddens.

Quickly, I say: "My dad said, 'Zane-boy, try everything. Food, games, skills. If it's new, try.' I tried oysters. I just didn't like them. But I like this." The sea. The boat. The strong, steady wind.

"Wise man, your dad."

"Was."

John's brows arch, but he doesn't say anything.

I quiet, overcome by sadness. Why didn't Dad take me sailing? Or oystering?

Maybe I'd have liked oysters better if I'd dug them myself? So many things we still needed to try.

I move toward the bow. After a few minutes, I feel Kiko behind me.

I don't turn around. "I miss him. Dad."

"I know." Kiko sighs. "I've got to ask. John, do you trust him?"

I turn. Over Kiko's shoulder, I see John and Jack laughing. "He's a character. Like Captain Maddie."

"And like Captain Maddie he's got a two-headed snake."

I bite my lip.

"I'm not stupid, Zane. You asked me to hide the cane's handle. But right on John's left hand is a ring that looks the same—a two-headed snake. Didn't Captain Maddie say, 'Beware the two-headed snake'?"

"Maybe she meant *some*? Beware *some* who carry the two-headed snake."

"So, great," says Kiko, sarcastic. "*Some*. But maybe she's the one who isn't trustworthy?"

"No, she wanted me to have the map. Wanted me to help her."

"So, what's the connection with the two-headed snake? With John?"

"I don't know. We'll figure it out," I say, tired of bad news.

John calls, "A song, a song." His baritone soars:

Safe and sound at home again, let the waters roar, Jack.
Safe and sound at home again, let the waters roar. . . .

(Captain Maddie's song.) "There's nothing to worry about, Kiko."

"Sure, there's not," she says, sarcastic. "Only stealing oysters."

"We won't do it. We're just researching. Trying to figure out a clue."

Scrambling aft, I join the sing-along:

Now we're safe ashore, Jack.
Don't forget your old shipmate
Faldee raldee raldee raldee rye-eye-doe.

John jostles me. "There you go, Zane. Pirate to the core. Where'd you learn the song?"

"A friend taught me."

"Ahhh." John's eyes narrow; his expression, grave. He looks toward the horizon. We're bobbing atop the waves. He cackles sharply; his lips stretch into a wide, toothy smile. "I had a friend I sang this song with. She was my best mate. Small bit of a woman but fierce. She'd drink gallons of rum and never spend a day hungover."

Kiko strokes Hip-Hop, checks the backpack. It's closed and safe.

"You're all too young to know about hangovers. Don't drink. Certainly, don't drink and drive." He cackles again. "Or sail."

"Are you really a pirate?"

"Ah, Jack, that I am. There are all kinds. Good ones. Bad ones." His voice lowers. "Loyal. Disloyal. But I'm sure your friend was splendid. A righteous captain."

"How'd you know she was a captain?" Kiko asks.

"Why, Zane told me."

I flush, remembering.

John leans in, his face so close I can smell his stale breath. "For a woman to be a pirate, she has to be the best of the best. Couldn't imagine you, Zanc, not knowing anyone but the best people. Am I right? Am I right?" He leans back. "Tell me I'm right."

"Yes. Captain Maddie was our boarder."

"You miss her?"

My feet shuffle. (It's too upsetting to talk about the captain.)

"I don't think she'd want us to steal oysters. Seems . . ." I struggle for the word.

"Petty? Small?" chortles John. "You're so right, Zane. Oyster pirates are scum. Real pirates—"

"Hunt for treasure?" asks Jack.

"So right, Jack. So right. To live the pirate life is to embrace adventure. The thrill of the hunt. The search." John stretches his legs, leans back against the bow, eyeing us.

"Are you three adventuring? Is that why you've come to the city?"

We look uneasily at each other.

"Is that why we're oystering? Not really for oysters. But, maybe, for treasure?" He slaps, rubs his hands together.

I squirm uneasily.

"Ahhh, I knew it, Zane. Share a story with your new friend John."

Kiko shifts, demanding, "You said 'miss her.' How'd you know Captain Maddie was gone? Dead?"

"Arrgggg." John's face twists with rage.

I blink. In less than a second, John's expression becomes calm. His eyes, kind.

Ignoring Kiko, John leans forward. His hands clasp mine. "I knew she must be dead because I heard the longing in your voice, Zane-boy."

I stare at the boat's bottom.

"Like the longing I heard when you spoke about your dad."

John's sympathy unsettles me. Kiko scoots closer, tapping me with her knee.

Brow furrowed, John leans back, both hands on the rudder. His face bland, he watches us. Waves lap against the wooden hull.

I'm confused. Comforting, the boat rocks, the sky is bright blue, and seagulls dive. But my gut feels tight; the back of my neck tingles. I'm confused, too, by Kiko. She stares at John, suspicious, tense.

"Hey," yells Jack, "that boat is moving fast. Look. It's headed right at us."

"Can't be," answers John. "Poor sailing."

"Jack's right," I holler. "What's the matter? Can't they see us?"

The boat is sleek, twenty feet long. Four guys without life jackets stand as it bounces, making waves. Our boat rocks with the shifting currents.

"Hold on," I shout.

John shifts the rudder. The sail deflates.

"What're you doing?" screams Kiko.

We're not moving. We're still, dead in the water.

"If we're not moving, it's easier for the boat to avoid us."

"I don't think so," I yell, standing up. "It's like they don't see us." Arms high, I wave my hands. Kiko and Jack join, shouting, "Watch out," "We're here," "We're here."

The boat moves relentlessly, thrashing up spray, foam.

"Rattler," I gasp. He's steering the boat. Bandanna kid stands right behind him. The other two boys I don't recognize.

"It's the crew that attacked us." Jack balls his hands into fists.

"How'd they know we were here? Sailing the bay?" wails Kiko.

The motorboat engine rumbles louder.

"Let me hold your backpack," insists John.

Me, Jack, and Kiko brace for a crash.

"Give me your backpack. I'll keep it safe."

"No, I got it," yells Kiko, slipping it onto her back. Her hands grip the mast.

"Hip-Hop. Heel." He sits beside me. I pat his head. "Good boy," I murmur, worried I can't protect him.

"Brace yourself," bellows John.

I want to close my eyes. But I don't. I can't believe Rattler's so calm. So careless. He's going to sink the boat.

A minute, maybe two until impact.

Rattler grins. Suddenly, sharply, he steers right. Gallons of water splash into the boat.

Kiko screams. Unbalanced, one side of the boat tilts deeper into the water.

The motorboat circles us.

"You want to fight?" dares Jack. "You want to fight?"

"That a boy, Jack," John applauds.

Hip-Hop, wet, whines as he's tossed like a toy dog.

"Respectable pirates don't taunt," John roars, raising his fist at Rattler and his crew. "Come aboard for a fight."

"No," I holler. "We've got to escape. If they were going to hit us, they would've done it already."

But John and Jack aren't listening. They're fixed on the circling boat, daring, "Come aboard and fight."

"No," I exclaim. If they come aboard, we'll lose the backpack.

I move to the rear, grip the rudder. The boat swings wildly around. Sails flap, billow from the wind angling across the bow.

"You'll have us overboard," shouts John. "She's a skiff, she's got no keel."

"Then help us," Kiko pleads while I urge, "Sail, John. We've got to sail."

He hesitates for a moment, then quickly adjusts the sail and helps me with the rudder. "Aim left; keep it steady, boy."

"We're moving," screams Kiko, holding Hip-Hop.

Wind pushes the boat. The motorboat keeps circling. But its trail widens, skimming into a larger oval.

"Move, move," I cry. "Move out of the way."

We're sailing but not fast enough. But because we're moving, the pirate crew can't board the boat. Jack's still raging. Kiko's protecting the cane and treasure map.

Rattler is now tailing our boat, edging closer and closer, gunning, then leveling the engine. Almost like he's going to ram us.

John's hollering, "What do they want, Zane-boy?"

"Don't call me that."

"They'll stop chasing us if you give them what they want," he urges harshly. "You must have something."

I almost tell. I don't want Jack, Kiko, or Hip-Hop to get hurt. But Captain Maddie gave the map to me. Not anyone else.

Furious, I turn, standing, bellowing, "Go away!"

It was Rattler who gave Captain Maddie the black spot. Who killed her.

"Your fight is with me," I bellow. "I'm Captain Maddie's first mate. Leave my friends alone."

"First mate?" Rattler laughs, hysterical. His crew joins him. Chuckling, slapping each other on the back, pointing at me.

"Go away!" I scream, trying to drown out the sounds of the waves, the motorboat, and the wind. The harsh laughter. "Go away!"

Rattler aims, speeds up, pushes the throttle. His boat jerks, leaping slightly out of the water, slamming down. *Smack. Splash.*

A wall of water rises, slaps, and I topple overboard.

Saved

"**Z**ane. Wake up."

My eyes won't open. My throat hurts. I'm drowning. I shiver in darkness, chilled to the bone.

My lungs fill with water; I feel the weight of it, pulling me down. Deep, deeper. Skeletons rise to meet me. Some wave; others circle me. Still others float, vacant sockets studying me as I drift farther and farther into the deep. Captain Maddie watches.

Why isn't she helping me?

"Zane, please. Please wake up. Zane, please."

It's Kiko, her voice high-pitched. Panicked.

"I told you we should've taken him to the hospital."

"He'll wake soon enough."

Who's that?

"Come on, Zane-boy."

"D-D-Dad?" I stutter.

"Zane. Open your eyes. It's me, Jack. Kiko's here. John, too."

"John?" I open my eyes. Kiko and Jack are by the bedside. John, the bell-bottom man, stands behind them.

"Where am I?"

"John's apartment. He saved you," insists Jack. "John saved you."

Kiko frowns. "He should've taken you to a hospital."

I sit up. "Heh." I'm dressed in loose black pants and a puffy pirate shirt. "Where's my clothes?"

"Drying," answers John. "Don't you remember? Falling overboard?"

"John dived in and saved you! You should've seen him, Zane. Not a second thought. Off with his shoes, then a sleek dive. You should've seen him."

"You must've been knocked unconscious, Zane. You didn't struggle," says Kiko, her voice strained. "Or try to float.

"We were really scared," she murmurs, wiping her cheek. (Is Kiko crying?)

Hip-Hop jumps out of her arms. He licks my face, then settles beside me, his chin on my arm.

I scratch Hip-Hop's ear, trying to remember: a circling motorboat, Rattler steering. John shouting, Jack daring. Water cascading into the boat. Hip-Hop soaked.

"The backpack?" I holler.

"I've got it."

I exhale. The map is safe. "Thanks, Kiko."

"I think you kids need help," says John, sitting behind Hip-Hop, across the bed from Kiko and Jack.

Baring his teeth, Hip-Hop shifts closer, like he's trying to protect me.

"Sssh, Hip-Hop. I'm okay." I embrace him tight.

"John's right," insists Jack. "We need help. You were doomed, Zane. He saved you."

"I did save you," John says, slapping the bed. "Felt as though I was losing a mate, a midshipman under my care."

Scowling, Kiko flounces from the room.

"Thanks, John."

"No worries, Zane-boy."

Strange. John's deep bass sounds like Dad's. Except he's got an accent that comes and goes. He sounds like he's from a Caribbean island no one knows about.

"Saving you was the least I could do. If I had a son, your father would've done the same, no?"

"Dad helped everybody."

"Especially kids," says Jack. "Your dad was cool, Zane. Cool like John. And he cared about kids."

"Adults are supposed to care for kids. It's their job," says Kiko, striding back into the room. "Sorry, Jack. Your dad is just bad at it."

Jack scowls.

(Jack's home life is complicated, I know. His mom though always waved to me.)

"Here's your clothes, Zane." Kiko lays my jeans, shirt, and socks on the bed.

"Get dressed," says John, emphatic. "We'll discuss later how I can help." He bows, flourishing his hand. "At your service."

"Let him have some privacy," says Kiko, shooing Jack and John from the room.

The two leave, their arms slung about each other. Jack's hand reaches up toward John's neck; John's hand effortlessly wraps around Jack's shoulders.

Kiko rushes back to my bedside, whispering, "We should leave, Zane. Soon. I don't trust John."

"John? He saved my life."

"I don't care. Neither does Hip-Hop. He doesn't trust John either. Has he ever let you down?"

I stare into Hip-Hop's soulful eyes. I'd give anything if he could talk. Treasure hunting is hard. Me almost drowning proved that.

"Nothing ever gets easier, Hip-Hop," I say, pulling on my T-shirt. "Losing Dad proved that."

"That's why you have us. Me and Jack."

I don't say anything. (Maybe friends aren't always enough?)

Kiko leaves, slamming the bedroom door.

Unsteady, I finish dressing. "Kiko's probably right, Hip-Hop. John's a strange character. You agree?"

He barks.

"But I almost died. At least, that's what Jack thinks. I don't remember falling. Or being in the water. I remember Rattler. Me yelling. Then cold, slippery darkness."

Sitting on the bed, I pull on my socks. I shiver, thinking how having two parents made life easier. I fall back on the bed, staring at ceiling cracks.

"I've got to find the treasure. Else Ma will lose the house. We'll have to leave Rockaway. I'll miss my friends. Hip-Hop, you'll have fewer treats."

He yelps.

I flip onto my stomach, stretching toward Hip-Hop. "Just kidding. You'll always have treats."

He whimpers, licks my nose.

"Yeah, I know. I'm sure Ma's worried sick. But I can't go home without treasure.

"How could it hurt to get help? Jack's right. John saved me." I prop myself onto my elbow. "I might've died. That counts for something, doesn't it, Hip-Hop? He saved me."

Hip-Hop jumps off the bed, scratches at the door. I wonder if he wants us to just leave the bedroom or leave John?

I open the door, seeing Zane, Kiko, and John. The room is shocking. It looks like Captain Maddie's room. Maps on the wall. A telescope. Two huge pirate flags—one red, one black. Except John's decorations are bonkers.

He's got Pittsburgh Pirates pennants. Movie posters of *Hook, Treasure Island, Pirates of the Caribbean*. Jack Sparrow's black-lined eyes glare. A skeleton with a red bandanna stands near the window, holding a skull-and-crossbones sign.

There's a wooden trunk, too—a dress-up stash, overflowing with hats, bandannas, white pirate shirts and black cotton pants, old muskets, rubber knives and swords. In the far corner is another chest stuffed with gold, silver, and copper coins.

"Money from all over the world, Zane. Can you believe it?" Jack digs his hands into the coins. "Captain John is rich."

"Captain John?" I echo. Like Captain Maddie? Saying "Captain" aloud makes me miss her more. I can't shake my sadness.

Jack, though, is the happiest I've ever seen him.

Kiko is definitely unhappy—no, not unhappy—mad. She's got the same simmering look as when she talks about Jack being his dad's punching bag.

"Look at this, Zane." Jack whisks off a red-and-white tassel-fringed cover. In a gilded cage is a black, beady-eyed parrot. (Alive, not stuffed.)

"Pieces of eight," caws the bird. "Pieces of eight."

Jack cracks up.

"Let me introduce my mate, Captain Flint."

"Captain Flint," mimics the bird. "Captain Flint."

"He's from Papua New Guinea," says John, his fingers stroking the parrot through the bars. "Most male and female parrots are the same colors. But Flint is an eclectus. Bright green like all the males."

"What color are the females?" asks Kiko.

"Red and purple."

"Sounds prettier," quips Kiko.

"Oh, no. Captain Flint is the handsomest. Best parrot ever. Better than the Veracruz Mexican parrots, or the macaws of South America, or the African grays."

"Have you been to all those places?" asks Jack.

"Indeed I have." He grins, expansive. "Some I toured with my old friend Captain Maddie."

I'm shocked. "You *knew* Captain Maddie?"

John opens the cage. The parrot steps lightly onto his hand, walks up John's shoulder, screeching, "Pieces of eight. Pieces of eight." The bird snatches a strawberry from John's hand.

"Captain Maddie and I hunted treasure. Do you hunt treasure? Search for precious goods?"

"Why didn't you tell me earlier that you knew Captain Maddie?"

"Sometimes I forget." John shrugs. "But I never forget about treasure."

"Just tell him, Zane," urges Jack. "He doesn't need the money. Do you, John?"

"No. Mind you, it's about the hunt. The discovery to be enjoyed."

"Yeah. And we need the help. John rescued you from the water, brought you to his apartment. Isn't this great?" Jack asks, arms outstretched, marching around the room. "It's clean, beautiful, not like my folks' shady mobile home." Snatching an apple from the bird's platter, he plops into a velvet chair. "I've never known anyone who didn't need money. If I had all this money—" Mind racing, he can't speak.

I look more closely. John's home is more luxurious than Captain Maddie's old room. Plush red velvet sofa and chair cushions. Silk drapes. Paintings line the walls—ships sailing through dark storms; or skating, bobbing over deep-blue waves; or anchored, a black-and-white pirate flag flying, while a crew loads crates. Blue-and-white porcelain vases, a cast-iron teapot, and crystal glasses sit on mahogany tables in the living room. Captain John seems richer than Captain Maddie ever was. But everything seems staged. Not unkempt or used or useful like Captain Maddie's books, jars, and maps.

Jack pleads, "This is our chance, Zane. Being poor sucks. Just tell John. Tell him everything." He leaps from the chair, eyes burning, repeating, "He saved you." He swallows. "He cared for you."

"He should've taken you to the hospital."

"I told you, Miss Kiko, after my years at sea, no one

understands drowning better than me. I'm expert at rescuing boys."

Again, John is answering Kiko but looking at me. "Zane's fine. Aren't you, Zane?"

I'm confused. John and Captain Maddie were friends?

"How'd you meet Captain Maddie?" Kiko asks, suspicious.

"For adventurers, the sea is actually quite small. Aren't you an adventurer, Zane?"

"*I* am," boasts Jack. "And Zane, guess what . . . John told me that since forever, Jack's been a nickname for John. Isn't that something?"

John pulls Jack close. Captain Flint squawks. "We're already friends," he says, squeezing Jack but looking at me. It's odd that he's looking at me again.

I start pacing, feeling like my head and heart are going to burst.

"Kiko—"

"No, Zane." She slips the backpack onto her shoulders, keeping the cane safe, tucked top down inside it.

I pace some more. Hip-Hop trails, turning when I turn, pacing back and forth, too.

What's the right decision? I wish I could ask Captain Maddie. She'd want me to trust her old friend. Wouldn't she?

"Didn't your dad say, 'Try. Try everything'?" John extends his hand. "Even friendship?"

I shudder, closing my eyes. Dad was friends with everyone.

"If he was here, what would he say?"

"He's not here," I mutter.

"Wouldn't he want you to provide for your mother? Your friends?"

"Let's get out of here, Zane."

"Kiko, stop."

Brows crinkling, I try to think. John's funny-looking, loud, and outlandish, but he hasn't hurt me or my friends.

"He wants to help," I insist stubbornly. "We couldn't have gone oystering without his boat."

"Oh, goody!" Kiko says, sarcastic. "So, you wouldn't have almost died."

"But he didn't," blasts Jack. "Kiko, your family's got money, so you don't understand anybody else needing it."

"Not true. Rockaway families are hurting. I *know* that. Still, we've got to be careful."

"Of what?" hollers Jack.

"You're so immature! You don't know anything."

"Stop it, both of you. I'm sick of your squabbling." Worse, I'm sick of being uncertain. Unsure of what to do.

Twice, we've been attacked. No, *I've* been attacked. Jack and Kiko are in danger because of me.

I pace. Hip-Hop sits, ears up, his head following my every move.

Jack frowns.

Kiko, gripping the backpack straps, studies the floor.

"What would *my* good friend . . . *your* good friend Captain Maddie say?" John asks, intent, unexpectedly blocking my path.

On his shoulder, Captain Flint balances on one foot. "Pieces of eight. Pieces of eight."

"What would Captain Maddie want?" he asks, sympathetic, compelling.

I feel waves of regret. *Watch for any strangers.* I wasn't a good lookout. *Seafaring boys.* I missed seeing Rattler as a danger.

"I was her first mate," I say. I don't say: *I failed her.*

"Now the captain's gone. Steer true, Zane-boy."

I shiver.

"You don't want to be blown off course."

John extends his hand. Captain Flint steps daintily down his arm, into his palm. He cradles Flint, stroking the feathers on his head. The slow, steady strokes are mesmerizing.

Captain Flint swoons, leans his tiny head against John's chest.

I try to stay focused on John's eyes. "Are you really a captain?"

"From the old school. Like your Captain Maddie."

I wince.

"You need help, mind you. The best adventures are shared." He points to Jack and Kiko. "You've got great mates. But you need a captain. Someone with experience and history. That's what you need, no?"

I shiver as if I'm beneath water again. As if a prize is just beyond my reach.

What would Captain Maddie want? Finish the hunt? Claim the prize?

I blurt: "There's a treasure map."

"Zane, no!"

"We need help, Kiko."

"But not his."

"I'm proud of you, Zane-boy."

"Zane-boy" makes me miss Dad even more. If he'd been alive, Ma never would have rented rooms. Captain Maddie never would've died in our house.

"A son recognizes when he needs a father's help. So, too, seamen. Explains why a first mate relies on their captain. Out at sea, far from home and shore, it's the captain who's father to all."

John is big, grown, and strong.

"We need help, Kiko," I say, decisive, firm. "We don't have to do everything on our own. Jack's right. It matters that John saved me."

"Yes, yes, I did," says John, boasting, slapping his chest.

"Matters that he knows adventuring."

"Yes, yes, I do."

Arms embracing, John pulls both me and Jack close against him. "My crew. My mates. My boys."

Captain Flint squawks, "Pieces of eight."

"But Captain Flint and I don't need a share. Do we, Captain Flint? It's kindness. Loyalty, mind you. I'm loyal as any father. As loyal as Zane's father would want me to be." He hugs me tighter.

"Give me the cane, Kiko," I urge.

"You'll have to take it, Zane. I'm not giving it to you."

"Pieces of eight."

"You're a spoiled brat, Kiko," Jack shouts, furious. "You think you're so smart. So special because your dad's got money."

"Don't be mean, Jack," I urge.

I reach for the pack. Kiko backs away.

"*Really*, Kiko?"

We stare at each other. We've been best friends forever. I extend my arm, palm open. "Please?"

Grimacing, she tugs the backpack off her shoulders and slams it to the floor.

Stooping, I snap open the clasp. Pull out the cane.

Awestruck, John reaches for the cane. He grips the handle. His two-headed snake ring matches the cane's brass snakes.

"See," he says. "Maddie and I were connected. Two heads looking out for each other."

I exhale. I'm making the right choice.

Pulling the cane back, I twist its top. Unlike John's large hand, the snake heads fit uncomfortably in mine. I clasp the joint throat.

No give.

"Harder," insists John.

Strange, the handle seems stuck.

"It wasn't hard before," says Jack, surprised.

Grunting, holding tight, I twist. *Nothing. I see Captain Maddie, hands on her hips. Watching, her eyes, blistering.*

The snake heads burn. I snatch my hand away. "Treasure. I need it," I say, desperate, unsettled. "Please. I need it for Ma. For our home."

Amazingly, the handle twists easily. Jack and John don't seem to notice. Kiko, on her knees, strokes a panting Hip-Hop.

I hold the cane upside down.

The map slips out like melted butter.

Captain Maddie disappears.

Revelations

"Seeing this map reminds me of good times," says John, rubbing his palms. "Sailing the high seas. Journeying, trolling for treasure."

We're all studying (even Kiko) the aged, yellowed map spread across the table.

John is expectant, eyes intent; Jack, ecstatic, glows; and Kiko's angry.

My hands shake. I can't help but think: this is my future—a musty sheet of thin, silky paper. Tracing the landmass with an empty harbor, clustered buildings, railroad tracks, everything seems compact, tiny.

"Totally cool," marvels Jack.

"It's Manhattan," I tell John. "See, it's surrounded by water. This is where the Atlantic merges with the Hudson River. Saltwater meets fresh. We think this is the harbor, the town."

"But the scale is off," says John.

"That's what we thought. The train tracks, too, don't make any sense."

"And there's no X marks the spot!" Jack complains.

"It's not true geography," says John. "Mind you, it is and it isn't. Early maps were often different."

"How?" I ask.

"They were focused more on the mapmaker's perspective about what was important. See. Manhattan has only a few landmarks. A port landing, a town, tracks to mark a journey, then a cemetery."

"Oh, oh, I get it," says Kiko, "the rest of Manhattan didn't matter. The story fits the hunt."

"Yes," I say, "me, Jack, and Kiko think *this* is Treasure Island."

"It makes sense," says Jack, lifting Hip-Hop.

"So right." Delighted, John smacks the table.

"This settlement must've been important, too. See the houses." Not looking at me, Kiko's nails tap the map. "Just before the cemetery with its tiny graves."

"Thanks, Kiko," I say.

She shrugs. "I want to find the treasure, too."

Quiet, we stare. Hip-Hop sniffs dust. Captain Flint, with four toes (two toes forward and two toes backward), steps carefully around the map's edges.

"Captain Maddie was wise to hide this," says John, his eyes wide, stroking the map. "Treasure's not meant for everyone.

"This ship"—his finger gently pokes the drawing—
"is a pirate ship. Sailing north to Manhattan."

"That's what Kiko thought."

John smiles. "Smart, smart Kiko. Maybe too smart?"
A brow arcs.

Kiko frowns.

I'm confused. Should I defend her?

John bursts out laughing. "No such thing! You need
wits to be a treasure hunter. Good for you, Miss Kiko.
These sails are fit for speed. Racing with cargo to
market. That's a pirate's life.

"See here. Tiny squares. Portals for cannons. Pirate
ships are always well armed. But less top-heavy for
stability. Arggh, I miss my ship. Once, I sailed the globe.
All I've got now is my skiff."

John's misery is real. Having lost his ship, he's
stuffed his apartment to the gills like Captain Maddie.
I feel closer to him. Not plain John, but Captain John.
I think he'd understand my fear of losing my home.

"This ship doesn't have a skull and crossbones,"
says Jack.

"But it has a black flag," replies John. "A not-so-
subtle warning."

"What's it mean?" asks Jack.

"'Give no quarter. No mercy.'"

Frighteningly, John's gaze freezes. His body stiffens.
It's as if he's remembering something dreadful.

"Do you think there's any connection between pirates and the skateboard crew?" I wonder.

"Wannabes." He slaps his thigh, coming alive. "A skateboard only sails so far. Just kids. Bullies."

"Aren't pirates bullies?" asks Kiko.

"There's a code of honor. Even among pirates. Most real pirates are retired from the seafaring life."

"Aren't there modern-day pirates?"

"Smart, smart Kiko," John answers, sounding more displeased than pleased. "South China Sea. East Africa. Caribbean and South American coastlines. So-called 'pirates' are on the rise. But they're thugs and thieves, plain and simple."

"Aren't all pirates thieves?" presses Kiko.

"No, more like forgotten heroes."

He paces like me.

"In the olden days, they were oppressed working men. Former slaves, the disenfranchised. Trying to survive in an unjust world.

"In the olden days,"—he continues pacing—"there was loyalty to each other. Swords, hand-to-hand combat." He pretends to stab a sword through the air.

"Didn't you say pirate ships had cannons?"

He ignores me.

"Pirates only took from the rich."

"Like Robin Hood?" asks Jack, gleeful.

"Yes, yes." John crisscrosses the room, his face aglow,

his voice commanding. "Today's pirates are ruthless kidnappers. Attacking cruise ships, mind you. Cargo ships. Blackmailing governments, corporations. Ransoming people. Ugly business."

"Not sure I understand the difference," snaps Kiko, scornful.

"The difference is romance. Glory."

"Glory," echoes Jack.

"Surviving turbulent seas. Swashbuckling. Youth admiring you and wanting to be a pirate. Experience freedom."

Kiko rolls her eyes.

"To be uncommon in a common world. A risk-taker. A new kind of hero," John booms.

"Like Jack Sparrow?" asks Jack.

Kiko bursts out laughing. "Ridiculous."

"Is not!" yells Jack.

"'In the olden days . . .' What days were that, John?" asks Kiko. "Are you a vampire pirate? Living forever?"

Roaring angrily, Jack lunges. Defensive, Kiko kicks up the cane, snatching it from the air.

Quickly, I step between them.

"Stop!" I shout. "Just stop." My head is hurting again.

I inhale. *Steer true.* That's what Captain Maddie said before she died.

"We need to focus," I insist, touching the map. "So,

this is New York. Long ago. When pirates—" I look at John, repeating emphatically, "Pirates with swords ..."

John nods.

". . . sailed the seas."

"So right, Zane-boy. North American pirates sailing to New York. A place for reinvention."

"Not easy for escaping slaves," mutters Kiko.

Jack's finger traces the sketched ship and miniature houses. "Wow, pirates lived in New York. It must've been a great port for discovering treasure."

"You mean stealing," Kiko mutters again.

"Yes, Jack, that's the pirate spirit." John clasps his hands to his chest. "A boy after my own heart."

"Give me a break," snarls Kiko.

"We're getting off track," I say, flipping the map. "Do you know what this means?"

John gasps.

Railroad Agent, the North Star

His expression goes blank, his finger lightly brushes the words. Then he straightens. "Railroads and ships? Nonsense."

(I'm confused. I don't believe John means what he says.)

I read:

One: Set sail. Gold is black; black is gold. Red is always red.
Port City landing. A wooden wall becomes a market.

"You said it yourself, John. 'Port landing.'" I tap the
dock. "Wall Street, the city's market for slaves."

Jack's palm covers the smallest stick figure. "No one
should harm a kid," he says softly, fiercely.

"Not ever," I answer, squeezing his shoulder.

"I need a swig." John grabs his flask off a table. He
half chuckles, lifting the flask like a salute. "Rum helps
set the mind straight."

Me, Jack, and Kiko glance uneasily at one another.

"Alcohol turns my dad into a wild man. You aren't
going to be wild, are you?"

"Wilder than I already am? No, no. What's the next
clue?"

I read:

Two: Oyster man, scoop from sand. Eat.
Pirates raid the black pearls. Stow the shells, stow the meat.
Beware. Two-headed snake.

John's right hand covers his ring.

"'Beware.' Doesn't that mean you?" asks Kiko. "You're
wearing a two-headed snake."

"So I am," John answers, swiftly lifting the cane.

"And Captain Maddie walked with one, gripping the snake heads in her hand. Keeping the map safe from murdering thieves.

"Beware." His voice deepens, his eyes bulge, and he sways like a barker before the haunted house.

Fearful, we pull back. Captain Flint flies into his cage.

John bellows: "Two-headed snake. A mark of loyalty, mind you. Everyone beware the two-headed snake. Four eyes to watch and two tongues to strike against betrayal."

"Scary," says Jack.

John chuckles. "Sacred is the bond between pirates. Loyalty. Loyalty, Miss Kiko. Loyalty, Jack."

Kiko crosses her arms; Jack nods.

"Zane-boy," John towers over me.

I try not to flinch.

"Two snake heads, better than one. Better to protect each other."

"Yes, that makes sense."

He hugs me, smelling of sweat, rum. I feel comforted yet uncomfortable.

"Like us, Zane-boy. We make sense. Captain and first mate to help one another." He takes another swig, wiping his mouth with his sleeve. "To the oyster man, too!"

"Not oystering?" I ask.

"No. 'Man' is the real clue. 'Oyster man.'
never taken you out onto the water."

"Or almost gotten him drowned," snar

John ignores her. "History, I told you
the 1800s, New York was famous for oyst
famous oyster man? The free son of slaves
dramatically, shouts, "Thomas Downing

We startle. Hip-Hop barks.

"Thomas Downing in a skiff, sailed
digging on the coastline, dredging for o

"In basements throughout the city,
oyster bars. Most were dark, slapdash.
peting with street vendors, struggled to
'Oysters,' they called, 'Five cents a doze

"Downing built his bar more like a res
every luxury. White tablecloths. Velv
drapes. Wall Street, mind you. Captair
sailors, bankers . . . the richest men
oysters and briny stew.

"And Miss Kiko, you'll like this——Do
women. Society women. Not songbir
ladies of the night. Businessmen wer
their wives to the elegant, respecta
Oyster House!

"Lit red lanterns meant he was op
Preparing, serving juicy, tasty oysters

"And Captain Maddie walked with one, gripping the snake heads in her hand. Keeping the map safe from murdering thieves.

"Beware." His voice deepens, his eyes bulge, and he sways like a barker before the haunted house.

Fearful, we pull back. Captain Flint flies into his cage.

John bellows: "Two-headed snake. A mark of loyalty, mind you. Everyone beware the two-headed snake. Four eyes to watch and two tongues to strike against betrayal."

"Scary," says Jack.

John chuckles. "Sacred is the bond between pirates. Loyalty. Loyalty, Miss Kiko. Loyalty, Jack."

Kiko crosses her arms; Jack nods.

"Zane-boy," John towers over me.

I try not to flinch.

"Two snake heads, better than one. Better to protect each other."

"Yes, that makes sense."

He hugs me, smelling of sweat, rum. I feel comforted yet uncomfortable.

"Like us, Zane-boy. We make sense. Captain and first mate to help one another." He takes another swig, wiping his mouth with his sleeve. "To the oyster man, too!"

"Not oystering?" I ask.

"No. 'Man' is the real clue. 'Oyster man.' If I'd known, never taken you out onto the water."

"Or almost gotten him drowned," snarks Kiko.

John ignores her. "History, I told you I knew it. In the 1800s, New York was famous for oysters. The most famous oyster man? The free son of slaves." John pauses dramatically, shouts, "Thomas Downing!"

We startle. Hip-Hop barks.

"Thomas Downing in a skiff, sailed the harbor, digging on the coastline, dredging for oysters.

"In basements throughout the city, people opened oyster bars. Most were dark, slapdash. Owners, competing with street vendors, struggled to make a buck. 'Oysters,' they called, 'Five cents a dozen.'

"Downing built his bar more like a restaurant. With every luxury. White tablecloths. Velvet chairs and drapes. Wall Street, mind you. Captains, merchants, sailors, bankers . . . the richest men swallowed his oysters and briny stew.

"And Miss Kiko, you'll like this—Downing allowed women. Society women. Not songbirds, theatrical ladies of the night. Businessmen were able to bring their wives to the elegant, respectable Downing's Oyster House!

"Lit red lanterns meant he was open for business. Preparing, serving juicy, tasty oysters. Fried, pickled, stewed, baked, and raw! Downing invented oyster stuffing.

"Imagine it, Zane-boy. 'Try,' as your dad would say. Imagine, a wealthy Black businessman when most Blacks were poor or enslaved laborers."

"Maybe there's a picture?" Jack flips pages of his "borrowed" book. "It's him!"

I stare: Thomas Downing, in profile. High cheekbones, receding hairline, gray beard, and an unsmiling, serious gaze.

Oyster King is typed beneath the portrait.

"If we'd read this first," says Kiko snarkily, "we wouldn't have needed John's help."

"But I like helping, Miss Kiko. I'm a modern-day Downing. A free man. Entertaining and helping his friends."

Downing reminds me of a preacher with his high collar and black cravat tied on a white starched shirt. In comparison, John seems garish in his striped pants, his gold chains glinting. Locs swaying, John moves boldly, sure like a man who shouts orders at a ship's crew.

But it's Downing's vibrant brown eyes that hold me. Even in a picture in a book, it feels like he *sees* me.

"Downing seems kind," I say.

"Says here he shipped pickled oysters to Queen

Victoria. She gave him a gold chronometer. What the heck is that?" asks Jack.

"A watch. The Rolex of its day. Worth a fortune then, worth two, maybe three fortunes now."

"'When he died,'" Jack continues reading, "'the Chamber of Commerce closed Wall Street.' On a weekday," he yelps. "They stopped making money so they could bury him? Unbelievable."

Kiko pokes Jack.

"So, the treasure clue is about Downing," I say. "But what're the 'black pearls' that 'pirates raid'?"

"That I don't know." John sighs.

"Pirates *do* raid," replies Kiko.

(I think: despite what John says, the skateboard crew tried to raid our map.)

"Pearls are treasure," I say. "Black pearls, I don't get."

"Black pearls are rare, found in Tahiti," John explains. "There, when an intruder, be it a grain of sand, a sliver of food, gets inside the oyster, the creature secretes fluids to protect itself, transforming the irritant into a beautiful black pearl. The oyster inside stays alive. Keeps safe enough to survive. Amazing. Turning nasty threats into beauty."

"*Pirates of the Caribbean*," muses Jack. "The *Black Pearl*. Wasn't that the name of Captain Sparrow's ship? Maybe the treasure is millions of pearls?"

"*Curse of the Black Pearl*," counters Kiko. "The movie was about a curse."

"So?"

"Keep to the clues, Jack. Downing must've been key to both oysters and pearls. He ran an oyster house, feeding people on Wall Street. Slaves were sold on Wall Street, brought to New York in ships."

"Pirate ships, right, John?" needles Kiko. "Did they sell human beings? How noble is that?"

"Kiko, you can be a pain," Jack says, exasperated.

John boasts, "Pirate life was a route to freedom. Mates, dark and darker than me, found family, a brotherhood."

"Yeah," says Jack.

Kiko snorts.

"Quiet, everyone. Let me think." I pace, trying to connect my thoughts. "Cargo. Transport. Pirates. Slaves. Oysters. Oyster meat."

"Don't forget shells," quips Kiko. "My dad crushes oyster shells to fertilize his garden."

Dumbfounded, we stare.

"He gardens, too?" I squeak.

Kiko shrugs. "Peonies."

(From pirates to peonies.) I pace.

We're all stuck. John rubs his head; Jack's left foot taps.

Kiko looks to me as if to say, *"Now what?"*

Frustrated, I say, "We can't keep outrunning the skate crew. Eventually they'll steal the map, find the treasure before we do."

"But you've got *me*, Captain John. I can take you there."

"Where?"

"To Downing's Oyster House."

"Why didn't you say so?" I ask.

"Yeah, why didn't he?" Kiko whispers.

"Give him a chance," says Jack.

John peels a banana for Captain Flint. He gives Hip-Hop beef jerky.

Hip-Hop gulps it down. Captain Flint mashes with his beak.

John walks to the apartment door, opening it. "Coming?" he asks, hands on his hips.

Jack swipes strawberries, bananas from Captain Flint's platter. He hurries forward. Kiko goes next. I smile. Kiko's got the cane again, safe in her backpack. I walk last.

"Proud of you, son."

John's gaze is mysterious. Not like Downing's clear, calm vision. Or Dad's loving gaze.

I keep moving, feeling both anxious and sad.

John locks the door behind me.

13

Hiding in Shells

We're back on track! Treasure hunting.

Me, Jack, Kiko, and John stand on the corner of Broad and Wall Street. The north-south heart of the Financial District.

Young businessmen and women with computer bags stroll, drinking Starbucks, checking phones. Older men with peppery hair stride, quick and straight like they own the world. Tourists meander, staring at guidebooks and buildings. Or else buying from carts bottles of water and bags of sugar-coated peanuts.

I check the streets. No sight of the skateboard crew.

John proclaims, "Here is the engine of capitalism, mates." He points to a heptagon building, built with limestone and marble. "Now owned by J. P. Morgan, mind you. America's first and most successful financial powerhouse.

"But," he turns, his voice rising dramatically, "before

Morgan, Thomas Downing owned all this, expanding his business to multiple buildings. Owned almost the entire street. A Black entrepreneur seeking treasure. Like a pirate, he found riches, money for his family, by lifting from financiers' and shipowners' pockets."

"Didn't learn this in school," complains Jack.

"More to life than school, Jack. The sea is the best education. Better than any book."

"Captain Maddie had dozens of books," I say.

"They teach us a lot." Kiko pulls out the library book. "We could've read this instead of listening to you."

"What do you think?" John asks Jack.

"I like your stories better! Downing must've been *really, really* rich. A millionaire."

For Jack, money's always important. It *is* important, I think. But what happened to Downing's family? Are they still rich? Is there a book about that?

Dad worked two jobs—selling insurance and doing house painting on the side. Before we had boarders, Ma sold holiday pies. Blueberry and strawberry for Fourth of July. Pecan and apple for Christmas. Sweet rhubarb for Valentine's Day. Now the house they worked so hard to buy might be lost. Rich? Me and Ma won't even have a home.

"I want to go inside," insists Jack.

"A true treasure hunter. Onward. No more talking."

Kiko rolls her eyes.

With Jack in tow, John marches up the marble steps. Security guards flank the huge wooden double doors.

I hang back. So much history on Wall Street, I think. Another way of saying "So many people dead."

I hear: the *tap-tap-tapping* of a cane.

"Captain? You here?"

My stomach constricts. *Am I dreaming again?*

I tense, a bit frightened. If Captain Maddie's spirit is here, she'd never hurt me.

"Dead don't stay dead." Her dying words.

Is this what it means to be first mate? Connected to my captain in life and in death?

Sunrays shining bright through clouds fade, darkening the sky. Surroundings lose color, becoming gray, black with dulled shades of white.

I turn, feeling the moist air, hearing a rush of whispering voices. History comes alive.

"You okay, Zane?" asks Kiko. "I knew we should've gone to the hospital."

No longer day but night. Gas lamps whoosh, flickering alight.

Jack, John, Kiko, and the guards disappear.

At the entrance, a Black man in a black silk suit with a white cravat climbs the steps. Thomas Downing?

Behind him, well-dressed businessmen and two women in feathered hats follow, chattering.

Two waiters wearing black pants, white aprons swing open the massive front doors.

Downing looks back, waves. "Come one, come all. Finest oysters in town."

One man shakes Downing's hand; the other pats his shoulder.

Before the doors close, Downing steps left, looking around the building's edge, down the street, before hurrying diners inside.

"Did you see that?"

"What?"

If I say, Kiko will think I'm losing my mind. Maybe suffering a concussion?

I remember Captain Maddie saying, "The past is never past." All along she's been proving it, guiding me.

John and Jack are arguing loudly with the security guard. Jack's angry, hopping up and down onto his board. John's arms and hands are distracting, flailing, trying to be persuasive.

"Give me the flashlight," I say to Kiko.

"Where're you going?"

"Cover me. Come on, Hip-Hop." I set my skateboard, kick off, and sail down Broad Street, the building's east side. One long building, then two, three, a row of shorter, pressed-together buildings. Single doors, double doors; marble and gray exteriors/columns. Huge windows like a palace.

I blink. This is real. Old, but still beautiful. Ghosts are living here.

My board catches on cracks. Tripping, I leap off.

Hip-Hop sniffs a patch of dirt. Near the ground, embedded in the stone, is a black coal chute. (Dad taught me long-ago coal cellars fed furnaces that kept homes warm.)

The chute is oversized. Someone dug out surrounding stone, enlarging the opening.

"Connected cellars," I say to Hip-Hop. "Cool. Great for storage." I stoop, lifting the hinged door. "Oysters were delivered through here. Genius, Hip-Hop."

He barks. We both peek.

Dark, dusty, chilly. My eyes adjust. Black upon black. Gray upon gray. No other windows. Cellar like a horror-movie basement. Double concrete sinks. No furnace. Just damp air. Lingering salt, brine. Vinegar? Crates, boxes, chairs. Dusty white sheets. Old barrels. Shelves upon shelves lined up like rows in a library. Some with ceramic casks.

I sneeze.

The basement is stuck in time.

Oyster shells are still in the chute.

Hip-Hop growls.

"No," I holler as he jumps through the chute. I hear, then see snatches of white fur as Hip-Hop searches, sniffs among stacked crates.

"Rats," I complain, climbing after him. Spiderwebs brush my face. I shine the light. No rats.

The floor is almost invisible, covered with cracked oyster shells that have been stomped into the earth. The sink is filled with brushes, knives frozen in a dried layer of mud. Bugs scurry. Rats could be anywhere.

"Darn it, Hip-Hop. Come here. Come."

He doesn't. Instead, he whimpers, his nose pushed between boxes.

I walk past rows of shelves. I pick up a ceramic container, wiping away decades of dust.

FINEST OYSTERS
THOMAS DOWNING
EST. 1825

I keep walking. The aisles between shelves go on forever. A dark, endless cellar.

Creepy.

Hip-Hop's scratching startles me.

"Find any rats?"

His ears flatten.

I pat his head. "No worries. Help me. There're secrets

here. Oystermen. Oyster shells. The answer to the clue must be here. I know it."

Hip-Hop bounds ahead.

"Hip-Hop!"

He yaps excitedly. Fierce, he digs as if bones were buried behind a slatted crate.

Dig-dig-dig.

"What is it?"

Dig-dig-dig.

I shove the crate aside, gasping.

Hip-Hop dives before I can catch him. He's through the tunnel.

"Come back. Hip-Hop!" I climb into the tunnel. I feel squished, claustrophobic.

"Hip-Hop, I'm going to get stuck."

My heart races; it's hard to breathe. I keep squirming, using my elbows like hands, my jerking legs like feet. The flashlight is useless.

"Oww." My jeans rip on a jagged rock. I feel blood on my thigh. Angry, I yell, "Hip-Hop. Hip-Hop! Hip-Hop!"

I burst through the tunnel, tumbling down. Air's punched out of me.

Hip-Hop licks my face.

"Bad dog, Hip-Hop." Warily, I stand. "Some kind of room," I mutter. But I can barely see. Here, dust, darkness, and webs are worse. I cough.

My foot kicks metal. I stoop. "It's a lantern." My fingers scratch the dirt. "Matches." Long, old-fashioned sticks.

I scratch one against the metal. *Zzzzz.* The flame flickers. "Please. Let there be oil." The wick glimmers. Then glows.

I raise the lantern.

"Unbelievable," I exhale. It's a cell. Bunched in corners are frayed, torn blankets. "Some kind of bedding?" I lift a blanket. "Eww." I drop it. Roaches scramble.

"Zane! Zane." Worried shouts.

"Zane? You all right?" It's Kiko and Jack.

Happy, Hip-Hop spins in a circle.

"Did you find the treasure?" John calls.

"Here. Here," I holler through the tunnel. "Down here. The south end.

"Show them, Hip-Hop." He dashes, races back through the tunnel.

I hear Kiko: "Hip-Hop. Is Zane okay?"

Then I hear John and my friends scrambling, crawling through the tunnel.

John curses. "I'm too big."

Kiko drops down and forward rolls. "Wow, what is this place?" She digs into her backpack.

Jack tumbles out, smacking his cheek on the dirt.

Kiko snaps on a flashlight. I light another lantern.

John, grunting, falls, collapsing headlong.

Panting, Hip-Hop leaps out of the tunnel onto and off John's butt.

I grin. "Good boy, Hip-Hop. You guided them through."

Not happy, John glares.

"Hip-Hop discovered this room," I say quickly.

Expression unreadable, John scans the small room.

Me, Kiko, and Jack (even Hip-Hop) wait for his reaction.

John scowls, disgusted. "There's nothing here."

"No, you're missing it, John. People, people must've stayed here." I touch the walls. "These plastered shells reinforce the walls. Making it more like a room. The shells would've added soundproofing. They're kind of beautiful, too."

The lantern's light makes the shells silvery, sparkling.

"Wish they were diamonds," growls John.

"There's buckets for water."

"Or worse," snaps Jack.

I ignore him. "This bucket has leftover shells."

"So, they were fed," Kiko muses.

"Feels like a cell," says Jack. "Prison lockdown."

"No," I say, pacing the area. "It feels more like a hideaway. A secret."

"Secret?" repeats Kiko. "Like stowaways?"

"On a ship, stowaways are put to work," adds John. "Else no water or food."

"But why hide people? Who'd hide them?"

"Oyster man," Kiko recites, "scoop from sand."

"Thomas Downing. 'Scoop from sand.'" Above and below," I add, excited. "'Eat.' It means upstairs, in the restaurant where the rich, well-connected, ate. Downstairs, the—"

"Poor," says Kiko, dumping oyster shells from the bucket. "Hungry, starving."

"Not just poor. Slaves."

Kiko gasps.

"This has nothing to do with treasure!" bursts out Jack, kicking a metal bucket. "This is a bust."

Hip-Hop scratches furiously at the wall.

"What're you doing, Hip-Hop?"

Yelping, Hip-Hop darts to me, then back to the wall, gashing, spraying dirt and shells.

"Give me the cane."

I grasp the cane, hitting the handle into the wall. More dirt scatters, falls. "It's another tunnel," I say, using the cane to widen the hole.

"Amazing," shouts Jack. But it's John who rushes in first, crawling through the tunnel.

Jack follows. Then Hip-Hop. Then me. On hands and knees, I twist my head, looking back.

Kiko's still standing, stubborn, stone-faced.

"I can't do this without you."

Grimacing, she slips off her backpack, pushes it into the tunnel, and follows.

Another underground room. Similar, craggy, luminous, shell-covered walls. Almost half the room is filled with metal tools, and shackles and chains rising against one wall.

"Definitely slaves," I say.

"Definitely treasure," insists John. "Here."

We spin around. Behind us, against the back wall, is a large chest.

John tugs at the enormous lock. "Bring me a cutter."

Me, Jack, and Kiko are spellbound.

"Hurry," shouts John, stretching out his hand. "Don't be slow, mates. The prize awaits."

Jack hands what looks like oversized metal pliers to John.

He squeezes with both hands, trying to cut the lock. "The prize is almost won."

"Diamonds," says Jack.

"Rubies," adds Kiko.

"No, silver. Or gold. Just like in storybooks," I murmur. "Hidden treasure."

Another deep heave. The lock snaps.

Jack reaches forward.

John slaps his hand away. "It's a captain's task to reveal bounty." Slowly, ever so slowly, he lifts the treasure chest's top.

"Aahhh," he exhales, then bellows, "Aargh. Damnation."

"A bust," howls Jack. "Nothing but a bust!" He slams the wall, sending shells flying. "Stupid, stupid bust."

"Calm down, Jack."

"You calm down, Kiko. Treasure doesn't matter to you." He squats, furiously pounding a fist into his hand.

Slumping beside John, I stare inside the chest. Empty. Except for dust, splinters of wood. Nothing valuable.

John's anger has weight. Like his entire body has turned to stone; his gaze is vacant and empty.

"Wait," I say. My fingers feel the bottom's corners. I press against the wood, comparing the level inside with the outside. "It's not deep enough. Maybe a false bottom?"

"Are you serious?" asks Kiko.

We're all on our knees, straining to see, hoping for a miracle.

My palm slaps downward. A spring releases. Wood gives.

Lifting the false bottom, I exclaim, "Another box. A small, pine treasure chest."

John quickly grabs the box.

"Open it," insists Jack.

I see some charms, talismans.

"A gold coin." John bites it. "It's real. But what good is one?" he snarls, standing, turning, banging the wall like Jack.

I hold a wood-carved canoe with a tiny figure inside.
"What's that?" asks Kiko.

"A man, I think." I twist the carved figure, trying
to stand him, but his feet aren't stable.

"Why's he flat? Lying down," I breathe. "Why not
carve him sitting? Rowing the boat?"

I lift a scroll, pulling one thread of the tied twine.
The paper unrolls.

"It's a note!"

Kiko hushes me with a finger to my lips. We read:

To T & G.D.,

> *Treachery on the North Star.*
> *Two souls dead. I'll be the third.*
> *Keep the cargos safe.*
> *Secure the gold. Keep the trains running.*
> *Until all are free.*

Agent E.

A clue within a clue.

I hear, "Who's down there? Is someone down there?"

"Turn off the lights," John urges hoarsely.

Quickly, Kiko puts the scroll, coin, and carved boat
back into its box.

Pitch-black, the cell feels creepier. I hear everyone breathing. Hear Kiko's backpack being zipped.

Beyond the dirt rooms and tunnels, walkie-talkies *crackle*. A man's voice, "Chute should be shut. Have someone check the inside door."

"We've got to get out of here. Blow out the lanterns in the other room."

"Miss Kiko should go first," urges John. "She's quick."

Kiko climbs through the narrow tunnel, her jeans and sneakers brushing, scraping. Following her sound, me and Hip-Hop crawl next. John and Jack are behind us.

"Trespassing," someone shouts. "Call the police."

"Must be the homeless," says another.

"Doesn't matter. Still a crime."

"It's disgusting down here," says a fourth voice.

Kiko has blown out the first room's lanterns. Me and Hip-Hop drop into the room, then stand, letting our eyes adjust to the dark. Through the first, narrower tunnel, we can see shadows, piercing flashlight beams.

"We've got to get out before we're completely trapped."

"We need to dash. Overrun the crew with force," whispers John. "Distract them."

"Are you sure?" I ask, anxious, disturbed I can't see John's face.

"They can't catch everyone, Zane-boy. Steady on the horizon."

Surprisingly, he embraces me.

"First mates don't go down with the ship. You and Kiko go first."

I swallow. The hug has caught me off guard. I don't know why, but it scares me. I try to pretend it's Dad encouraging me.

"What if someone's still outside?" Kiko murmurs. "On the street?"

"Hip-Hop can chase them," I say, hugging him tight.

"Police are on their way." A voice warns. "Give yourselves up!"

"Zane, you and Kiko go left. Jack and I will decoy, going right. We'll double back after you escape."

John sounds like a captain, strategizing, saving his crew.

"We've got guns," another voice shouts.

"Guns?" Kiko squeals.

"Don't think about it. Just go! Now!" orders John.

"Hip-Hop's behind you," I tell Kiko. "We can do this!"

We crawl, faster and faster through the tunnel's darkness. Dirt flies from above and below. I hold my breath, trying to keep from coughing.

Kiko drops from the tunnel's edge. Hip-Hop whines. I fall forward.

We stand, gasping. Lights blind us.

Men yell: "Stop," "Don't move," "Police are coming."

"Go!" I shout, pushing Kiko.

She runs.

Hip-Hop barks. I shield my eyes, running left.

The men give chase. Barrels and clay jugs break. Oyster shells spill, snap, crack as the men run over them. Flashlight beams cut, crisscross the cellar.

Clasping both hands, I make a step for Kiko to lift herself up into the chute.

"Hurry." I lift Hip-Hop. His nails scratch, *click-clack*, *clickety-clack*.

The men are closer. Close.

I'm not going to make it. With both feet, I spring, hanging desperately on to the chute's frame.

Someone grips my foot. "Got you!"

"Ahoy. Here! Over here!" It's Jack.

I kick. The man grunts, stumbles back.

I see lights shift, spotlighting John. He's like a circus performer, hopping, waving, taunting with boxing jabs. He's grinning. "Come fight me. Captain John."

Jack, beside John, is furiously pitching oyster shells. With a grunt, he throws his weight against a shelf filled with dusty jars, jugs. The shelf falls, crashing, shattering glass and ceramic.

Jack and John split, running in different directions.

Above, outside on the street, I hear Kiko scream, "Get your hands off me."

Hip-Hop growls.

A security guard yells, "Stay back." Then I hear running, barks receding as Hip-Hop chases.

I hurry, scrambling upward. The slippery chute is worse than climbing an oversized pool slide.

I see daylight, Kiko's face framed by the metal opening. She extends a hand, helping me climb out. I look down the shadowy chute hoping to see Jack. John.

Hip-Hop dashes back to us.

Kiko helps Jack out. We all stare down the chute, listening, looking for John. There's nothing except shadows and wands of light.

"He's trapped?" asks Kiko

"John!" I call, his name echoing over and over. "John!"

Hip-Hop sticks his nose into the chute. A sweaty, red-faced man with black eyes looks up at him.

Hip-Hop barks wildly.

I holler, "Run."

"Stupid kids, I'm coming out."

Sirens. I see red and blue twirling lights. One squad car. Two. Three.

"We've got to go," screams Kiko.

"Come on, Jack," I say, nervous, seeing a crowd gathering.

"We can't leave John."

A hand reaches out from the chute, grabbing Jack's jeans.

Kiko repeats, "We've got to go."

"Jack!" I clasp his shoulders. He shakes me away.

Sirens wail louder.

The guard, flailing at Jack, is half in and half out the chute.

Kiko drops her board. "John can take care of himself. Come on."

I unsling my board, too. "Jack, we can't go to jail."

The crowd is larger, rowdier. A businessman sneers, "Delinquents." A food cart worker shouts, "Thieves. Stealing from my cart."

"No, we didn't," I holler.

"Troublemakers," a red-faced man wearing a vest and bow tie says with scorn. "Where're your parents?"

"Jack!" I shout, frenzied.

He lays down his board, rolling behind me.

"Catch them," a woman with a red purse demands. "Catch them for the police." She swings her purse at Jack.

"Yikes." Jack dodges swinging leather, grasping hands, and the guard, out of the chute, running after him. The guard Hip-Hop chased is back, yelling, joining the chase.

"Sail!" I order. "Sail." *Stay focused on the horizon.*

We're off—sailing, tacking, and banking left and right, down congested Broad Street.

A patrol car, its siren on full blast, tries to maneuver through the packed street. Cars and taxis can't move.

I panic, hearing a motorcycle rumbling, the engine gunning.

"Split up. Distract, decoy!"

Kicking, legs stroking asphalt, we each shift, change direction. Our boards rattle; the wheels grind.

"Meet up at the church," I yell.

Exhausted guards and people have slowed. Squad cars are penned in by traffic. But the police motorcyclist *zooms* after Jack.

"Floor it, Jack!" I shout, banking right.

He raises his hand high.

He's on it!

Jack kicks his board forward. It rolls beneath cars as Jack leaps onto and across a taxi, black sedan, and Mini Cooper. He lands on his slowing board, kicks it into high gear, zigzagging north, then behind a limo, he sharply U-turns, cuts right, disappearing down a street as the motorcycle zooms by.

Grinning, I tell Hip-Hop, "Hop on." He does, and the two of us swerve right, whizzing (not as fast as Jack!) down an alley, across Broad Street until I can't hear any more shouting or sirens or motorcycle engines.

Me, an escaped criminal. Ma's not going to understand.

Would Captain Maddie?

Recovery

"Slowpoke," teases Jack.

Of course Jack got to the church before me!

Hip-Hop leaps off the board. I try to do a back-side powerslide, but it doesn't go smoothly. I trip, fail miserably, and have to catch myself with my hands.

Jack laughs, bends toward Hip-Hop. "High-five."

Hip-Hop taps his paw to Jack's hand.

"Traitor," I say, ruffling Hip-Hop's fur.

"Get off the street," orders Kiko, peeking around the corner from the church cemetery. "Follow me."

Kiko's right. The side cemetery is a smarter place to hide. To catch our breaths.

As soon as we're in the graveyard, Jack insists, "We've got to go back for John."

"No!" Kiko blurts.

"It's only fair, Kiko," I argue, but stop speaking,

stunned. "Where's the cane? You lost the treasure map?"

"John stole it."

"You're kidding," snaps Jack.

"Am not."

"Seriously?" I ask.

Lips pressed tight, Kiko nods.

My back against the church brick, I slide to the ground, holding my head in my hands. This is awful.

"You're wrong, Kiko," argues Jack. "John wouldn't steal it. He must've thought the map would be safer with him. And he was right."

Hands clenched, face red, Kiko exclaims, "*I've* got the map, Jack! I wanted to see who you trusted more. Me or John."

"What?"

Kiko reaches into her backpack. "See. I folded it."

Jack grabs for the map.

"No." Kiko quickly zips the map back into her pack. "I don't trust you. I was right not to trust John."

"Such an awful know-it-all! You're not in charge."

"Cool down, Jack."

"Tell Kiko to cool down. She's always thinking she's right. About everything."

"Because I am! You and Zane are too trusting."

"John," I insist, "was helping us."

"That's it, isn't it? *John*. You just wanted his help. You both desperately wanted it. That's what you agreed about—*his* help. *His, his, his*."

"That's not fair," I say angrily, standing.

"Both of you wanted"—she pauses—"a grown-up."

"You mean like a dad?"

"You said it, Zane. You've been missing him bad."

I can't speak, can barely breathe. (I do miss him.)

"That's the stupidest thing I've ever heard," scorns Jack. "I've got a dad."

"Who hits you!"

Furious, Jack turns away.

"You're friends," I holler. "Friends since elementary school. Friends don't fight."

Kiko sets down her board. "I'm sorry, Jack."

Jack still looks angry. His jaw and fists clenched. I clasp his shoulder; he brushes me off.

"She's *your* friend," says Jack. "I just went along." He lifts his board. "I'm going back to look for John." He stares fiercely at Kiko. "It's the *right* thing to do."

"Jack! Come on, Jack."

Me and Kiko trail behind him. He turns the corner, smacks down his skateboard, and does a rolling ollie over the steps, lands bold, knees bent, board perfectly flat. Perfect.

"Jack," I call.

He doesn't look back. Just sails, weaving through traffic, people. He speeds onward. Searching.

I slouch, returning to the cemetery. The landscape seems fitting. Death changes everything.

Casket, flowers, and dirt. Those are my last memories of Dad.

My knees up, leaning against the church wall, I stare at the headstones and monuments. Some are moss-covered; others cracked with age; some rectangular; others have crosses mounted or etched on stone.

Kiko sits, quiet, beside me. She breathes deep, unsteady.

Hip-Hop pants.

Mid-afternoon, the sky is darkening. Moisture from the harbor and bay dampens the air.

"I'm sorry, Kiko. I shouldn't have gotten you mixed up in this."

"Friends help friends."

"All I wanted was a happy adventure. How'd it get real so fast? So dangerous?"

"Everybody wants treasure."

"I just want to keep our home. Dad said owning a home mattered. He worked two jobs to pay for it. Said, 'Housing discrimination is real.' Said a house will always provide for me and Ma.

"If we lose it—" My breath catches, tears well.

Kiko looks away. "Solve the problem, Zane. That's all we've got to do."

"Yes. Connect the clues." I stand, staring at Hamilton's tombstone. It's bright, beautiful even. A rectangular base with marble urns on each corner. Rising above the base is a white stone triangle, reaching toward the sky.

"He opposed slavery. Died 1804."

I rub my head, pace. *Think, Zane, think.*

"Kiko, who built Trinity Church?"

"My phone's dead, Zane."

"You didn't bring a charger?"

"I forgot." She frowns, biting her bottom lip.

I don't say: "You never forget. *Anything.*"

"Dad's been texting. Calling. I turned off the sound. Should've turned off the phone to save the charge." Her brows rise; her eyes look bleak. "I think I wanted the phone to die."

"It's okay, Kiko. Mine's in my stolen backpack."

"We'll figure out how to call once we find the treasure! It'll be soon. It's got to be soon."

"Right." (I feel guilty, too. Ma mustn't think she's lost me.)

"I did text Dad to tell your mom, Jack's mom, we're all okay."

"Thanks, Kiko."

"Focus," murmurs Kiko. She closes her eyes. Concentrates.

"John said slaves built Trinity."

Her eyes fly open. "Slaves." She grips my arm. "Architects rented slaves! Slaves did the work, and their owners were paid. It all fits. Wall Street, forced, free labor."

I scan the cemetery. So many graves, all with their own stories and history. Who knew? Since sailing to New York, I've felt the past haunting my present.

"The treasure map shows people arriving on New York island."

"Hamilton came from Nevis, a Caribbean island," interrupts Kiko.

"Downing was from where?"

Kiko has the book ready. "Chesapeake Bay. Oyster country. The book says his parents were slaves freed by a sea captain."

I nod. "So he stayed in New York, built a business, made a home. Oh, oh, I understand." Bile rises in my throat. "Some Blacks are free. Some, slaves. Some, ex-slaves. Some—"

I look at Kiko. Both our eyes widen.

"Runaways," we exclaim.

"That's it, Kiko. New York had an underground railroad."

Kiko pulls out Agent E.'s note, unfurling it on top of a flat headstone, reading:

Keep the cargos safe.
Secure the gold. Keep the trains running.
Until all are free.

"Agent E. must've been a conductor," says Kiko.

"'Keep the trains running.' They were searching for freedom. Freedom trains. But not necessarily real trains. You could walk, run your way to freedom."

"Like Harriet Tubman." Kiko lays out the tiny treasures from the pine box. "You could also sail to freedom."

"Right, Kiko. The treasure map proves some sailed from the South to New York.

"So, 'cargo' must mean people." My fingertip touches the wood-carved boat, the tiny figure inside. "Runaways couldn't leave the ship as a group. They must've come into the harbor hiding, lying flat, in boat bottoms. That's why the figure can't bend or stand."

"The book says oystermen were mostly black or Lenape, native people. Zane, they must've been agents, too. The perfect cover. Transporting runaway slaves to shore. The oystermen would've understood losing freedom."

"And land. Home. Slaves lost their African homes. Natives lost their New York land."

"'Lost' doesn't seem like the right word," murmurs Kiko.

"Yeah, you're right. Stolen," I gripe. "Their homes were stolen. Just like developers are trying to steal our home, our community.

"Thomas Downing was an agent. Hiding runaways in his cellars. People must've been the 'black pearls' hidden in oyster-covered tunnels and caves."

"The note's addressed to 'T & G.D.' Thomas Downing!"

"'G.' I bet that's his son."

"None of Thomas's customers—the businessmen, rich people—none of them ever knew."

Kiko lifts the gold coin from the pine box. She holds it up to the sun. It glitters.

"Money," I say. "There had to have been other treasure. Owning slaves made you rich. Remember the first clue: 'Gold is black; black is gold.' Slaves as wealth. How disgusting! But there must've been gold, too."

"Right. 'Cargos,' *plural*. 'Keep the cargos safe.'"

"Smart, Kiko. Agent E. died conducting both runaways and gold."

"'Treachery on the North Star.'"

"Fighting. Betrayal," I say. "How awful."

Kiko unfolds the map.

We read together:

Two: Oyster man, scoop from sand. Eat.
Pirates raid the black pearls. Stow the shells, stow the meat.
Beware. Two-headed snake.

"I think it's talking about the oysters and slaves, at the same time. Hiding, stowing runaways, feeding them and the upstairs diners. 'Pirates'—"

"They must've sailed the ship. The *North Star*!"

"Yes. They must've been paid for transporting southern runaways. Maybe they wanted more?"

"Deliver the slaves but steal the gold meant to help the railroad and other runaways."

"Yes." I exhale.

"But what does 'Beware. Two-headed snake' mean?"

I step back, feeling uncomfortable. "I don't know, Kiko. I don't know."

On the gravestone, Kiko lays down the gleaming coin and lifts the map toward the sun and bright sky. The yellowing paper is thin, transparent.

Marveling, she murmurs, "I think there's invisible ink."

"You're kidding?"

"In science camp, I learned to make invisible ink using lemon juice. You can use milk, too. Either way, light and heat reveal the message."

I grab the flashlight. *Click.* Light beams through the fibers. Slow, ever so slowly, lines, curves, handwriting appear:

Three: Treasure buried.
Look to the spirits, the forever bones. Treasure lies within.

"Wow," I say, stunned. "Who wrote this? When? 'Treasure buried.' Reburied?"

"Yes, maybe. Hidden on ships. In canoes. Hidden on land."

"Secrets kept."

"Buried." Kiko flips the map over. "The cemetery."

The collection of tiny crosses mirrors Trinity's small cemetery and the old Rockaway cemetery where Dad's buried.

"For how long?" I wonder.

Hip-Hop paws at my leg. I lift him. "Hip-Hop knows about treasure. The backyard is filled with his buried bones.

"But these represent people. How many runaways stayed in New York? Built a community? Gave birth to free children? Lived and died?

"Thousands of Black people lived in early New York."

"Hundreds of cemeteries."

"But only one that holds the treasure," I marvel.

"Unbelievable, your Captain Maddie found the map."

"Skeletons and gold," I whisper, hugging Hip-Hop tighter. He trembles; so do I. "What a story. Secrets kept across time. Discovered, then rehidden. Not once but twice."

"Sunlight's fading," says Kiko, looking up at the sky. Clouds gather.

Breezes swish through leaves, trees, and graveyard grass. *A gust of wind.*

Kiko catches the map before it flies away.

"Captain Maddie?" I ask. Open-mouthed, Kiko stares.

Listening close, I hear bones stirring and clattering, eerie cries, and muffled wails. Kiko doesn't hear.

"Look."

"What?"

The map's cemetery glows. Tiny crosses blink like warning lights. Bright, then less bright. Pulsing bright, less bright.

"Quick. Give me a pen."

Kiko digs into her backpack. "Here."

"Connect the dots," I whisper. I press the felt tip, spreading ink diagonally. A solid line. At the top, another cross. I draw again. Another solid line piercing tiny crosses. Two diagonal lines crossing each other.

"X marks the spot."

"Wow, oh, wow. An optical illusion. Like the picture: Is it a vase or two faces?"

"A true treasure map! I wish Jack was here. He would've loved this."

Foreboding engulfs me. I look across Trinity's cemetery. Weathered headstones—names faded, some hardly readable. A copper statue turned green—a man no one remembers.

Finding treasure is meant to be thrilling, happy.

I didn't count on people chained and sold. Long ago, dead and buried.

Loss

"Good to see you." Ms. Gutiérrez, wearing more "READ" buttons than ever, welcomes me and Kiko.

"Where's your other friend?"

"Jack," I say, stressed. "He couldn't come."

"Can you help us? I'm Kiko. He's Zane. We want to discover where slaves are buried."

Ms. Gutiérrez stops smiling. "In New York, the United States, the entire world?"

"Here. In New York City."

"Serious research. There are internet and print resources."

"And maps?" I ask.

"Yes, maps."

Hip-Hop, from inside Kiko's backpack, tries to push his nose through the small, zippered opening.

"I didn't see that," sighs Ms. Gutiérrez. Thinking, she bites her lip, then exhales. "I have a study room

where you can work. But he'll—Hip-Hop?—will have
to be quiet."

"Got it." Me and Kiko grin.

"Black pearls, black pearls, black pearls," echoes in
my mind.

The room is windowless, safe. Ms. Gutiérrez didn't
ask any questions (and I'm glad). She just brought
research materials and gave us her lunch.

Hip-Hop snarfed a third of a ham and cheese sandwich. Me and Kiko shared the rest of the sandwich, a
dill pickle, and carrots.

Maps are strewn over the table. Kiko's head is buried in books. Stomach full, Hip-Hop sleeps, snoring
in the corner.

I pace around and around the small table. *Black
pearls, black pearls.*

"Didn't John say when oysters were attacked, they
created pearls? Beauty from struggle?" I blurt excitedly,
"It's a metaphor."

"So, you *do* listen in class."

"Always." I chuckle. "Black people are the black
pearls. Their own treasure. For conductors like the
Downings—"

"Or Harriet Tubman."

"—helping runaways must've felt like treasure. They
risked everything to save people's lives."

"That's good, Zane. Then there is actual treasure—gold coins, jewels, maybe. Pearls?"

"Buried with the black pearls? *One* black pearl? Or more?"

"Here," says Kiko, flipping pages. "Look at this." We stare. It's a photo of a federal park with a redbrick building, expansive trees, and a beautiful lawn. A towering stone marker, inscribed:

AFRICAN BURIAL GROUND
NATIONAL MONUMENT

"Acres and acres of bodies buried. It says here that in 1991, New York City was trying to build a skyscraper. Digging, they discovered the Negroes Burial Ground, created when America was a colony. For two—*two* centuries, Zane, Black people, free and enslaved, were buried here."

I whistle. "Thousands upon thousands of bodies. We've got to go there. Come on."

Hip-Hop wakes. Kiko grabs the backpack. All three of us run through the library. Hip-Hop's nails clatter on the linoleum. Readers, irritated, "sssh" us; some call, "No running."

Kiko turns back, waving, "Thanks, Ms. Gutiérrez. Sorry, too. We're going to find the dead."

Her brows arch.

"Kiko!" I cry. "Come on!"

Hip-Hop barks.

"You kids stay safe," Ms. Gutiérrez shouts, following us to the door.

Patrons loudly hiss, "Sssh!"

We're in the sun, our skateboards rattling. I scan the crowded streets. No one's watching us. Except Ms. Gutiérrez. She's still standing in front of the library, hand held high, waving.

It's a good sign, I think. People caring about one another is a good sign.

16

Buried

The walk isn't long, but it's hot. I'm sweating and my breath's ragged. Kiko holds her backpack like armor.

Feels like people rushing by are going to crush us. Everyone hurries, hurries, hurries. Jostling, running, bumping.

Hip-Hop growls, yips when people's feet tramp too close.

We're still in the northeast section of the Financial District. But moving farther north. Billboards. Neon lights. Offices. Restaurants. Tons and tons of frenzied people.

"Move aside, kid."

Pushed, I stumble, grip a lamppost. Astonished, I hear: *whizz, whizz, whizz.* It's a low rumbling I've heard before. Hair on my arms rises. I want to throw up.

The sound grows, builds—noisy, rattling wheels *whizzing* in unison. We're being hunted.

"Pirates," I yell. "Rattler and his crew."

Thundering, turning from the right and left streets onto Broadway, dozens upon dozens of skaters appear. They're following us. *How'd they know?*

"They've been spying all along," groans Kiko.

"Tracking us. Go, NOW, Kiko!"

We kick off on our boards, trying to avoid the shoppers, tourists. Stores are selling everything from clothes to cupcakes.

The road isn't better. Huge crowds cross against the streetlights; taxis honk; bicycle delivery riders act like daredevils.

Me and Kiko are daredevils, too. "Distract," like John said. Outsail. Outsmart. Twist down alleys, leap over steps, swerve and screech. Our boards are LOUD. The skaters behind us are LOUDER.

We head east toward the national park's burial ground. We're getting close. Closer. A huge monument surrounded by grass looms. One last street to cross.

Oncoming traffic, a Don't Walk sign, forces us to slow. Someone clutches my T-shirt. I swing my arm back.

"Get off me." I kick my board onto the street. Cars slam brakes, horns blare. A taxi hits the bumper of another.

Kiko screams.

Weaving, I nearly tumble onto a taxi hood. I dodge in

front of and behind cars. Angry drivers call me names. One last kick stroke, a pop up onto the curb.

I'm safely across, but Hip-Hop isn't.

"Hip-Hop, nooooooo."

He's so small, it's harder for drivers to see him. It's a one-way jammed avenue.

"Hip-Hop!" I couldn't stand it if Hip-Hop was hurt. Or killed.

Kiko clings to me.

I shake her off, stepping onto the street. I raise my hands like a crossing guard. "Stop," I order, my face fierce. "Stop." I glare at drivers. No one is going to hurt Hip-Hop.

"Sit, Hip-Hop. Sit."

I pick him up in the middle of the street. Hold him close.

A second ago, drivers were yelling at me; now they're applauding.

I smile. Who doesn't love Hip-Hop?

Safe on the curb, Kiko, crying, clutches us both.

On the other side of the street stands a grim Rattler.

Furious, I want to punch him.

His crew is laughing. The Walk sign lights up. But they don't move. They stand with one foot on their boards, mocking us.

"Is that—?"

"Aaargh," John cries out. "Go away, go away, vile crew. Captain John is here."

Stomping across the burial ground, John's coming toward us. Shaking the cane, yelling furiously at the hunting skaters.

I set Hip-Hop down, pick up my board, and run. Hip-Hop chases after me.

Kiko yells, "Wait."

I know Kiko's warning me, but I can't help myself. I run, relieved, grateful I haven't lost John. Dad, Captain Maddie are gone. Yet John's here. He found me.

I throw myself against him.

"There, there, Zane-boy," he soothes, patting my back.

Emotions overwhelm me. I want to give up, break down. Searching for treasure is too hard. Me, almost drowning. Escaping Rattler. Nearly losing Hip-Hop.

I step back. "I haven't lost you."

Feet planted, both hands clasping the cane's ivory snakes, John smiles.

My stomach unclenches. The sky brightens; the upside-down world is right side up.

John offers me the cane.

I hold it, feeling the slick wood, the cool handle. We're going to solve the clues, find the treasure! I just know it!

I look across the street. The pirate skaters are gone. Taxis are moving; the sidewalk swarms with people—office workers, tour guides, sightseers, families strolling with babies.

Dragging her feet, face unreadable, Kiko comes close.

I say, "John didn't get caught."

"Wish he had."

"Kiko!" I cry, appalled. (She's tough but never unkind.)

"I missed you, too," replies John. "I brought back the map, Miss Kiko. I saved it."

She reaches for the cane. "You didn't look inside?"

"No, why should I? The map is safe inside."

"See, Kiko, John wasn't trying to steal the map." He wasn't betraying us.

Hip-Hop looks at me, looks at sullen Kiko—back and forth, his gaze darts. Back and forth. He knows me and Kiko are out of sync.

John boasts, "I saved you from those pirates, too. With me here, they didn't dare cross the street."

Kiko scowls, holding the cane like she's going to whack John.

I grab her arm. "Focus on the clue, Kiko. Isn't that what you told me?"

"Ah, yes. Our purpose. Why are we here?" Gleeful, John rubs his hands together. "Treasure? Glorious treasure."

"Wait, did you see Jack? He went to find you."

John hesitates, then, slapping his thigh, says, "No. Can't say that I did."

Kiko freezes.

Grimacing, I feel guilty, angry at myself that I didn't ask right away about Jack.

But I was shocked to see John.

Another thought gnaws: *How did John find us?*

"Let's get to it," John presses. "Can't spend a lifetime hunting for treasure. Let me help. You'll all be rich. Isn't that what Captain Maddie would've wanted?

"Zane-boy, don't you want to make your ma proud?"

"Ma," I whisper. (I've got to get home.)

"We came to see the monument," I add, "because of the last clue. Kiko had the map all along."

Frowning, Kiko jabs me in the stomach.

"Ow."

"Miss Kiko still doesn't trust me? I'll remember that," John snarls.

I squirm—*sensing what?* I'm not sure. But both Jack and John have gotten so mad at Kiko.

"Kiko's great," I insist. "She only does what she thinks is best."

"As do I, young mate. As do I."

Inexplicably, John's words chill me. (What's he mean?)

"Let's go see the monument," John says, abruptly turning.

I can't see his face. I really, really *want* to see his face. It's as if I'm missing an important clue.

A clue to what?

I look back at Kiko. With her head down, I can't see her face either.

I'm surprised. Who knew hunting for treasure would feel so lonely?

The soft grass cushions my feet. Seeing green, growing trees, is hopeful. A park in New York.

Off to the side is a sign:

AFRICANS IN EARLY NEW YORK

A walkway leads to a huge, looming, black granite slab. Sunlight reflects off the shiny surface. Green bushes, plants and trees, the white clouds, and blue sky all enhance the blackness. The monument's beautiful.

"Over six acres of skeletons, decomposing bones," says John indifferently. "Miles of sea bottom, too, are covered in bones."

I wince.

"Poor souls," sighs Kiko.

I place my palms on the granite.

It feels electric—like the stone is alive, humming.

I read:

> For all those who were lost
> For all those who were stolen
> For all those who were left behind
> For all those who were not forgotten.

"Thousands hurt, murdered by the slave trade," I say sadly.

Throwing his head back, John bellows, "Millions! Millions, Zane-boy. Youth can't imagine the scale, the numbers lost, stolen, or left behind."

"But they're not forgotten," I respond, feeling hurt. "Isn't that the point? No one should ever forget?"

He cackles. "History is a poor teacher. Truth is— slaves *were* forgotten. It's the twenty-first century, mind you. What've you learned in school? If not for this treasure hunt, would you have thought about the past? Look around you. Who knows how many, let alone *who* the dead are buried beneath the city's roads?"

"The final clue said—"

"There was another?" John interrupts. He's so close I can smell his sweat, his stale, dry mouth.

Kiko elbows me again.

Smirking, John arches back. "Suspicious Miss Kiko. Mind you, Zane-boy, survival is all that matters. It'll become truer as you grow older. Survival is all that matters."

Strangers study us; some peek, some step back, avoiding us as John's voice grates louder and louder.

"Stop talking, John," hushes Kiko. "Be respectful. This is like a shrine. Peaceful."

Kiko's right.

I press my palm onto the marble. It's alive. Captain Maddie died talking about "bones people." Spirits that aren't gone. She told me Dad isn't gone. And I know he isn't.

I hear voices, echoing: *"Not forgotten, not forgotten."* Maddie's voice, too: *"Honor the bones people, whether buried in water or earth."*

For the first time, I feel connected to a history I'd known but hadn't thought much about.

Standing in front of the huge granite, I feel small. Small because there's a bigger history. Me, linked to Africans brought to American shores.

Pointing, I ask a park employee. "What's this sign?"

"*Sankofa*—a symbol from Ghana. It means 'learn from the past.' *San* means 'return,' *ko* means 'go,' and *fa*, 'look, seek, and take.'"

People gather round.

"This is the Wall of Remembrance. Sometimes Sankofa is drawn as a bird looking backward. Throughout the burial ground, there're dozens of symbols."

"You mean clues?"

"Yes, in a way," he says, eyes sparkling. His brows, black; his hair, speckled gray. "Follow me."

Everyone follows—twelve, maybe fifteen people. Some couples, some college kids, some children and their teacher. Only John lags.

On the monument's right side is an opening like a door. From this angle, it's clear the monument is not a flat slab; rather, it's a prism. Multisided with a narrow, triangular space built between granite.

"This is the Ancestral Chamber."

Inside, between sheer granite, the space and darkness are both scary yet soothing. We all move, single file, up the slope.

"We rise twenty-four feet to commemorate 'the door of no return.' The threshold where kidnapped Africans left forever their home, family, and tribe."

As we near the top, the light at the end of the chamber grows bigger, brighter.

"Hear the water?" asks the guide. "It's meant to be healing. Not traumatic like the Middle Passage, the captured Africans' journey across the Atlantic."

"My mom taught me about the Middle Passage," Kiko whispers.

We're out of the passageway, in the open air, feeling sunshine again. Single file, we step down the stairs. On the right is a small waterfall, and inches of water pool alongside the chamber's exit.

Others file out. Voices murmur and sigh.

Strange, I still don't see John. I nod at Kiko.

"The entire monument is symbolic of a ship," adds the guide. "We've left the ship's bow. Now we walk its deck—the Circle of the Diaspora. Twelve stones engraved with symbols. Each represents a different African culture."

I tread slowly, down the spiraling ramp until I reach a flat, circular floor with a map carved into the stone. "Is this old New York?"

"Yes, when there weren't any skyscrapers," replies the guide. "Follow me."

We keep spiraling down, descending even farther, way beneath street level. Going deep, deeper into the burial ground.

"This is Libation Court."

He quiets. Everyone else quiets, too. Couples hold hands. A kid with a book-heavy backpack frowns. Two elder women seem about to cry. No one looks at their phone or tries to snap a selfie.

I move closer to Kiko and Hip-Hop, feeling the coolness of stone dug into cooler earth.

"We gather here for sacred offerings." His eyes closed, palms flat and open, the guide stands tall. "In the Sankofa spirit, honoring past, present, and future generations."

I close my eyes, too, feeling my spirit float with wisps of air.

(I'm certain, more than ever, that Captain Maddie guides me. She wants me here.)

Still somber, people start to leave. Like each

person—the students with their teacher, the sweet-
hearts, the out-of-town visitors—knows when it's time
to go.

Me, Kiko, and Hip-Hop, though, don't move. The
tour guide leaves us, walking slowly back up the spiraling ramp.

Calm washes over me. More than ever I want to
make things right in the world.

"Kiko, I'm going to call my mom. Tell her I'm sorry
for worrying her."

"Good luck finding a payphone."

"When it's over, when we bring home the treasure,
do you think they'll understand?"

"Maybe. My dad is furious. He's probably called the
police."

"No way."

Kiko shrugs. "Yes way. But I couldn't let you treasure hunt alone."

"Jack came."

"Jack," she blurts, "isn't dependable. Neither is John."

I explode. "So, you know everything, Kiko? About
everybody? Jack's been my friend longer than you."
(Where'd that come from?)

Kiko's face reddens. She puts down Hip-Hop, then
spins, marches up the ramp.

"Kiko, stop." (What's the matter with me?) I shouldn't
be a jerk to Kiko. Even Hip-Hop doesn't look at me.

I run after her—up the spiral, past the waterfall, up the steps, racing down through the chamber to the narrow entry door.

I expect Kiko to throw down her skateboard, sail away. But she doesn't. She dashes toward the museum building.

"Hip-Hop, stay," I say as I chase her.

Inside the museum, I see exhibits, panels, paintings of the slave trade.

On my left, painted statues—a Black mother, father, child, chained—hold hands together.

I shiver. They look so real.

On the wall, a huge screen plays video images: a construction site (on the top right corner, the year, 1991); African Americans protesting; construction stopped; archaeologists digging, uncovering coffins. Next to it is a drawing depicting layers of dirt with foundations and building materials from three centuries. 1700s. 1800s. 1900s.

I want to stop, make sense of what I'm seeing. But I've got to apologize to Kiko.

Ahead of me, the cane still in her backpack, she swiftly moves, turns a corner.

I race. I can't lose sight of her.

Her hand pushes a door marked Ladies. I hesitate. Pace back and forth. Back and forth. No one else goes in. Or comes out. I don't hear toilets flushing. Or taps dripping water. Just crying.

"Kiko!"

She's sitting cross-legged on the floor beneath the hand drier. "You shouldn't be here," she says, wiping tears on her sleeve.

"I'm sorry. A thousand times. More than you'll ever know. I'm sorry, Kiko. You're my best friend, just like Jack."

"You're really stupid, Zane. Jack can't be trusted. Neither can John."

I stare at her disbelievingly. "Where'd you get these thoughts?

"I want us to be like before, Kiko. You, me, and Jack. No fights. Just friendly teasing. Three forever friends."

She hesitates. "I saw Jack with the skateboard crew."

Stunned, I can't speak, think. I leap up. "You're crazy." The mirror reflects me—so frustrated, angry, sad. I want to smash something. Go back in time. Sail on my board. Time-travel. Go back three days—be with Jack and Kiko again at Rockaway Skate Park.

I inhale deeply. Exhale. Pace.

"I'm sorry, Kiko. I shouldn't have called you crazy. Jack's loyal."

"To himself. You don't see it."

The bathroom door swings open. "Oh, excuse me." A girl blushes furiously, then hurries out.

"We should leave," says Kiko, standing.

"Kiko, wait." I clasp her hand. "Did you ever like Jack?"

Her body rocks slightly, side to side. "Yeah, I did. But I liked you more."

"What?" I drop her hand, gulping, "You don't mean—?"

"Naw, I don't *like you* like you. Not like that. I just like you."

"Great. I mean—" Now I'm blushing. "Sorry. It'd be okay if you did. I wouldn't mind."

Kiko laughs, a big belly laugh. "You should see your face."

"Let's get out of here."

"Zane," she says as I'm about to push open the door.

I turn, looking seriously at Kiko. She looks miserable.

My voice cracks. "Are you sure you saw him?"

"I must've been mistaken."

I nod, not knowing what to say.

Walking quickly through the lobby (faster than Kiko), I feel upset, unsettled. My stomach's queasy. Part of me knows Kiko's trying to make me feel better.

Was that John's excuse? Was he trying to make me feel better, too? Saying he didn't see Jack?

Jack disappears; Captain John appears. How *did* John find us?

Kiko's always beside me. She wouldn't lie. She's loyal. I shake my head, trying to clear my thoughts. Follow the clues.

17

Mounds & Ghosts

Outside the sliding glass doors, Hip-Hop yips, greeting me. His stumpy tail wags.

"Good boy," I say, rubbing behind his ear. "Good, good boy."

Ears flat, he whines. Immediately dashes off, then darts back to me. Scratches my leg.

Feet firmly planted, fists on hips, John calls, "Mates! I thought I'd lost you."

"Had to go to the bathroom," I say, then, more directly, "Why didn't you visit the memorial?"

"Seen it before. Couldn't see how it would help me find the treasure. Not unless, mind you, you're hiding something? Are you?"

Hip-Hop scratches my leg. *Scratch-scratch.*

"If something's hidden, you're NOT supposed to know about it," replies Kiko.

"Aren't we all mates? Captain John and his loyal crew?"

"Stop it, Hip-Hop!"

He keeps pawing and pawing. Then he barks, rushes forward, spins, rushes back to me, barking some more.

"What is it, boy?"

"He wants us to follow him," says Kiko.

Over and over, he runs away, then back to me. Like the guide, he's leading us down a trail. We follow as Hip-Hop heads to the grassy area, left of the monument.

He sits, barks. Then howls. Eyes closed, nose pointing to the sky, he makes a wailing, mournful sound.

"Hey." I squat beside him. He lays down, sniffing the dirt.

Seven mounds. All in a row. Covered by grass.

"What's this?"

"Reinterred remains, mates."

"You mean they dug up and reburied skeletons?" asks Kiko, walking to a plaque. "Says here intact skeletons—four hundred and nineteen—were buried beneath these mounds."

"That's all?" (What happened to the others, their bones?)

I place my palms on the mound nearest me.

People wander. Talking, gazing. Some skirt around me. I don't care. I don't move. I can't. Just like the monument, it feels like the earth's electric, *buzzing*. Calling me.

I touch my forehead to the cool mound.

"What're you doing?" shouts John. "Stop this nonsense. Acting batty like a land-starved sailor!"

I sit back on my heels. "Gold was buried in the cemetery," I murmur. "In a coffin, maybe." (As soon as I say it, I know it's true.)

"Are you sure?" asks Kiko.

"Yes. These are the bones mentioned in the clue."

"What clue?" demands John.

"'Treasure buried. Look to the spirits, the forever bones. Treasure lies within.'" I look up. "It'd been written in invisible ink."

"Are you sure, Zane-boy?" asks John, on his knees, gripping my shoulders. "Are you sure?"

"Yes, all the clues lead here. To these graves. Thomas Downing aided the underground journey of runaways. When pirates betrayed him, tried to steal the gold, he buried it."

"With the dead? You're sure, Zane-boy?" Gleeful, John leaps up, clapping. "Such irony. Sweet irony." He claps again, doing a jerking jig. (Never mind he's dancing between graves.)

Standing, I feel overwhelmed. Dizzy. My head hurts.

Kiko's perfectly still, staring at the memorial park, the walkways, streets, skyscrapers, lampposts, and streetlights. The restaurants, delicatessens, banks, apartment and office buildings. A concrete world filled with hundreds of cars, buses, and thousands of people living—walking, riding, chattering.

"The original cemetery was more than six acres. The gold could be buried under that pizza shop or that bus route. Even under that hot dog stand. Manhattan on top of a cemetery." My stomach clenches. "I've got to see it. I've got to see."

"See what?" asks Kiko.

"Manhattan."

"We're here, mate. Are you mad?" asks John.

I look up. Building after building piercing the blue sky. Tall, taller, tallest. I'm dazed.

"From the sky," I say. "Skyscrapers."

I take off on my board, whizzing on the sidewalk, the street. Sailing where the channel is clearest—with fewer people, parked cars, trash bags, and buses. Up ahead, due north, I see a skyscraper. Not the largest, but the closest to the African Burial Ground.

The skyscraper is thick-bottomed with scores of windows. It narrows, three smaller tiers with spires, rising high, then topped with an oxidized green copper triangle with a balcony and birdhouse-looking windows. The copper tapers with elaborate shapes— curlicues, swooping panels, and ending with a sharp needlelike pole poking sky.

Me and Hip-Hop stop in front of the building.

"It looks like a cathedral," says Kiko, sailing up.

John, breathless from running, stops short. "It's the Woolworth Building. If you want a skyscraper, go to the One World Trade Center building blocks behind it."

"No," I say, staring up at a carved owl and an eagle, centered above the archway, the massive gold-metal-and-lead-glass doors.

A doorman stops me. "Son, you need a ticket to tour."

"We don't have any money," says Kiko.

The doorman shrugs.

"When was the building built?"

"1913. It was the tallest building in the world until 1930."

I turn to John. "I've got to go inside. Please, help."

"Why go inside? The truth's underground, isn't it?" John peers at me.

I can't explain. I just know I need to see Manhattan from high.

Click-click. I *see* the drawing in the African Burial Ground museum.

The higher the building, the deeper you have to dig. Dig, dig, dig. Disturbing hallowed ground.

I crane my head back. The concrete, glass, and steel building soars.

"Please. Help," I say to John. "I need to go inside."

"Twenty dollars for thirty minutes. The top floors are off-limits. They're residences."

John frowns.

"You said you wanted to help," snaps Kiko.

John pulls a twenty from his wallet.

"What about me?" fusses Kiko.

"No more," John sneers, pulling out another twenty. (His wallet is stuffed with bills.)

"Hip-Hop, wait with John."

He barks.

"I know. It isn't fair," I say, stroking his fur.

John reaches for Kiko. "Let me hold your backpack, the cane. Security might search it."

"Let them. I doubt they'll find anything." Kiko smiles tightly, rapidly blinking, fluttering her lashes.

Scowling, John crosses his arms against his chest. His fingers twitch, flex into fists. Instinctively, I step between him and Kiko.

Laughing, John throws up his hands. "Brave, Zane. I'm not going to hurt anyone. Especially a kid. Mind you, I'm a man of strong emotions. Miss Kiko knows I only want to help. You know that, too, don't you, Zane? You trust me?"

He smiles wide, his teeth bright, his lips stretched thin. Kiko rolls her eyes. I feel relieved. (Dad said, "Adults are supposed to help, not hurt kids.")

"Sorry, John," I blurt. (But part of me isn't sure. I'm confused again.)

I push the revolving door. "Let's go, Kiko." She follows.

I look back through the spinning glass doors.

Hip-Hop, his head on his paws, pouts.

John, his hands on his hips, stands tall, commanding. Unexpectedly, he winks.

18

High in the Sky

"The Woolworth Building, designed by Cass Gilbert, was the first skyscraper of the Financial District," says a red-suited tour guide leading twenty of us. "Mr. F. W. Woolworth owned a chain of five-and-dime stores. Known simply as Woolworth's. He built American discount stores before there was today's Dollar Tree and Family Dollar stores. This was his corporate headquarters."

Me and Kiko are awestruck. We're in a surreal world or a fantasy movie set of good battling evil. We stare at the soaring three-storied arched and vaulted entrance. The ceiling glows with pastel paints—clouds, soaring angels, sunrays. There're birds everywhere! Peacocks, owls (tons of owls!), sculpted, painted, or designed with brightly colored tiles.

"The flying phoenix!" heralds the tour guide, pointing at a panel of red-and-gold birds. "A symbol of Christian rebirth, resurrection."

"Money's not a religion," mutters Kiko, elbowing me.

"The elaborate neo-Gothic architecture was inspired by cathedrals of medieval Europe," says the guide. "The famous Reverend Camden nicknamed this headquarters 'the Cathedral of Commerce.'"

"For a dollar store?" I squawk.

The couple next to me and Kiko laughs. The tour guide frowns. A gray-bearded man, wearing a Cubs hat, insists, patronizing, "Woolworth's was the finest store of its day. Some had soda fountains."

(What's a soda fountain?)

I slowly spin about. Lobby walls are elaborately trimmed with carved walnut. Marble floors, gold lamplights and doorknobs. Mosaic trim. Stained glass. Colorful murals cover the walls. It's beautiful.

"What's up with the creepy gargoyles?" I ask, pointing upward at the leering, scary creatures.

The tour guide ignores me. I count over a dozen metal-forged gargoyles, projecting from the ceiling arches. I shudder. Grotesque, evil-looking faces, some human, some animal.

"Gargoyles on a church were meant to ward off evil," says Kiko. "Or to remind people of evil. I have no idea what they're supposed to mean here."

"Yeah. In an office building. A fantastical one."

"That's it. I knew I'd seen this headquarters before. In the movie *Fantastic Beasts and Where to Find Them*."

"Wizards? This adventure is getting weirder."

"You bet." Kiko punches me.

"Ow."

"This has nothing to do with the map. What're we doing here, Zane?"

"Looking for a way up."

"Why?"

I stutter, trying to express how seeing Manhattan from on high feels critical to the story. Past meets present. Mr. Woolworth's wealth built upon free labor. Slaves as currency.

"This way, please."

Like he's the pied piper, everyone follows. Feet shuffling, heads straining, up and back, side to side, everyone admires the lobby.

On either side of the hall are two large murals. Sweeping his hands to the right, the guide says, "This is *Labor*." Sweeping left, he proudly announces, "And this depicts *Commerce*. Both paintings a testament to America's entrepreneurial spirit!"

"Is it a sin if you don't make money?" I mutter. "Is that why the gargoyles are so frightening?"

Behind me, someone snarls, "Quiet."

Kiko sticks out her tongue. "Strange, sad. A business designed like a church."

"Ssssh," hiss tourists.

"Now something truly exceptional," the guide boasts.

"The Woolworth Building is entirely self-sufficient. It has its own power plants. President Wilson himself threw the switch on opening day, which turned on eighty thousand lights.

"Mr. Woolworth paid thirteen and a half million dollars. In today's dollars, that would be three hundred and seventy million."

"What happened to Woolworth's?" a girl with an I ♥ NY shirt asks.

"The chain went bankrupt."

"So much for entrepreneurial spirit," I snark.

"Let's get out of here," Kiko insists.

"No, wait. The guide's speaking."

"This building was sold in 1998. Now there are offices, a mixture of companies. On the very top floors are thirty-two luxury residences for the ultrawealthy. Penthouses in the sky."

I nudge Kiko. "That's what I want to see. Up, in the sky."

"The Pinnacle Penthouse occupies floors fifty to fifty-eight inside the building's copper dome. It has one hundred and twenty-four windows, nine thousand seven hundred square feet, and its own private observatory. Even its own private elevator," says the guide, standing before black filigree and gold-plated doors.

A sign on a golden stand reads: Beyond This Point, No Tourists Allowed.

"Does anybody live there?" I ask.

"No. It's for sale. Seventy-nine million dollars."

People in the crowd whistle, exclaim, chattering, "Who has that kind of money?" "Can you believe it?" "Seventy-nine million for an apartment? Unbelievable."

"Please, step this way," says the guide. "I'll share some design secrets."

"Come on, Kiko." I dash forward, press the private elevator button. "I've got to see."

"Hey, that's not part of the tour!" the guide shouts. "Security, security!"

The elevator doors open. I pull Kiko into the bright, mirrored space.

A guard rushing, running, shouts, "Get out of there. It's private. We'll call the police."

"Hurry, close, close, close!" shrieks Kiko, repeatedly pressing the P button.

The doors slide, then stop. The guard's hands clutch, push on the panels.

"No," I shout, startling the guard, using my skateboard to whack his hands away. Kiko presses P again.

The doors slide closed.

"Whew, we made it."

"We're in so much trouble, Zane."

"Feel it?" I ask.

"What?" Suddenly, she grips the gold handlebar. "Fast." Mirrors reflect her fear. "It's moving too fast."

"Feels like a drop tower going up!"

"Don't say that. What if it crashes down?"

I chuckle. "It's got to be fast to reach the fiftieth floor!"

We feel the elevator car slowing, slowing, stopping. The doors part. Even empty, the apartment's gorgeous. Brilliant white walls, white floors. Sunlight streams everywhere. Across the floor, the ceiling. A staircase in the living room's center spirals upward for five floors.

"Hurry, Kiko. They'll be after us. This way." I twist the levers on floor-to-ceiling glass balcony doors. They swing open.

We catch our breath.

Wild gusts of wind. Layers of pancake clouds. Shades of blue. A fierce ball of a sun.

Massive skyscrapers—steel, glass, concrete, polished stone—fill the island.

Awed, I exhale, "Unbelievable."

"It's New York."

"Look at that. Isn't that One World Trade Center? Must be over a hundred stories high!"

"A hundred and four floors. My dad and I visited."

"Incredible. I didn't understand, Kiko. Manhattan's an island of buildings. Buildings and more buildings everywhere. Mid- and high-rise businesses, banks, and apartments. Then soaring, gravity-defying, incredible skyscrapers."

"Hard to believe people can dream, create—"

"Build?"

"Yes, build such marvels. As if people were legends, gods."

"No. Just human." I grimace, staring at the blue-green horizon of rivers, harbor, and ocean.

Manhattan is just a sliver of land jutting into water.

Why doesn't it sink? Why don't all the people, the skyscrapers, weigh the island down? Sinking everyone, everything?

"We should leave, Zane. Guards will be here any second."

I bend my knees slightly. I balance my weight, solid between my feet. "We're standing on graves, Kiko. Can you *feel* it?

"Down, down through skyscraper floors, to its deep foundation into remnants of other buildings built atop mud, dirt, to a time when there weren't any buildings at all."

Kiko clasps my hand. "Just six acres of the African American cemetery."

(I remember planting flowers atop Dad's grave. I'd be heartbroken if someone laid brick, stone, concrete, and steel on top of him.)

"In 1991, one skyscraper gets canceled, Kiko. But not Woolworth's in 1913. Not any buildings built before. What did they do with the coffins, the bones? Mix them with stone, concrete? Throw them away?"

My outrage grows.

Click-click. In my mind, I *see* the treasure map unfolding in 3D. "X," I say, "This is X. X marks the spot. Woolworth's, densely packed stores, office buildings, and apartments, all of it is on burial land."

"Oh, Zane."

"The city built a monument—a museum and a memorial. Less than a third of the original six acres. The rest of the cemetery didn't matter. To anyone. For a long, long time."

19

Warrior Girl

"You two, get out of here."

Two burly men grip me and Kiko, steering, propelling us through the Woolworth lobby (the tour guide smirks!) and shoves us out the revolving glass doors.

"Next time, we call the police."

I trip, stumble to my knees. I grimace.

"Don't come back!"

Kiko stands defiant. "As if we would! This place is *aaawwwwful*. Even if it was in *Fantastic Beasts and Where to Find Them*."

"Stay out of here," barks a guard. "Go home."

People pass by—bored, oblivious, uncaring that two kids were thrown out of the Woolworth Building.

Uncaring that for over three centuries no one honored New York's Black buried dead. (Would it have taken as long if the dead had been white?)

I sit, cross-legged, on the sidewalk. People walk

around me. Boots, high heels, sneakers, flip-flops. Rock-away folks would've stopped, asked "What's wrong?" New Yorkers trudge on as if a kid plopped in the middle of a sidewalk is normal. Nobody cares.

I give up. Adventures are overrated.

Even Captain Maddie chose not to uncover the treasure. (Who says a first mate has to do what a captain didn't?)

"Zane, get up. You've got to get up." Kiko pulls me up. Her gaze tells me she's really, *really,* worried.

"Let's go home, Kiko."

"Really?"

"Yeah. Let's go home to Rockaway."

"Now you're talking! Dad'll be mad, then super happy. I miss him."

"I miss Ma, too. Hip-Hop," I call, scanning the sidewalk. "Hip-Hop? Where are you? Hip-Hop?" Panicking, my voices cracks.

"Huh. John's not here either. Not good. Hip-Hop," calls Kiko.

I whistle. Whistle again.

"Findley's got him." It's the spy kid with the bandanna and mirrored sunglasses. "Follow me." He crosses Broadway to City Hall Park. He stops at a huge, square water fountain. Water sprays, arcs from the four corners. A central waterfall with a bronze cross-like spike on the top spills water that flows from the square pool into four separate semicircular pools. Another time, I would've thought it was soothing. Kiko would've wanted to throw a coin and make a wish. But we're both too anxious.

Though I can't see his eyes, even the kid seems fidgety, nervous. He points to the tree farthest south from city hall's steps.

Pirates. Two taller, older boys, lanky, dressed in black, sneer. One straddles his skateboard; the other twirls a sack. Something scratches desperately, trying to get out.

"Hip-Hop!" I run, lurch forward, trying to rescue him.

The second boy shoves me.

"Let Hip-Hop go," Kiko screams.

"Ransom is the pirate's way," says the redheaded boy holding Hip-Hop in the sack. "I'm Findley. This is Matt. Rattler's mates. If you want your dog, give us the map."

Hip-Hop snarls, whines.

"And don't say you don't have a map. Our crew isn't stupid."

The other kid sniffs, wipes his nose with his arm.

"Findley and Matt are serious," says blue-bandanna kid with sunglasses. He steps closer, his voice high-pitched. "They're going to hurt your dog. I don't want no dog hurt."

I see a terrified me in the mirrored sunglasses.

"Well, ransom or not?" Findley holds the sack high, above his head.

Hip-Hop's barking, his body wildly twisting, trying to escape.

"I could just drop him. Like this."

I gasp.

Hip-Hop yelps. At the last second, Findley catches the sack. "You're cruel," screams Kiko.

I lunge, furious.

Findley swings the sack behind his back.

Matt grabs me, twists my arm. My knees buckle. He punches, kicks me.

I crumple.

"Treasure map for the dog," Findley taunts.

"Please don't hurt him," I beg. "You can have the map. Anything."

"Stay back, Zane. I've got this." Kiko's jaw is rigid, determined. Casually, she slips off her backpack and calmly lifts out the cane.

"Kendo is the 'way of the sword,'" she says, grasping the cane with both hands. "Discipline, moral spirit are more important than fighting."

"Good," says Findley. "This island belongs to Rattler and our captain. Pirates control the seas, these streets. Any treasure is ours.

"Pay the ransom. This stupid dog won't get hurt. Won't be thrown overboard."

"No," I shout. "You can have the map. Don't hurt—"

"I've got this, Zane."

"Hear that? The girl's got this," hoots Matt, sarcastic.

Hip-Hop snarls. But inside the bag, he's moving less.
Can he breathe?

"Kiko, give him the map. We don't need it. Let's go
home."

Body at ease, knees bent, Kiko's focused. In the zone.
I've seen her practice kendo on my porch hundreds of
times. Before she simply battled air. Swiping, angling
at no one.

"Quit, Kiko. I don't want you hurt."

She ignores me. Cane tilted on a diagonal, eyes fixed
on Matt and Findley, she says, "Boys first."

"Get her, Matt."

Matt sniffs, swings.

"Kiiiii—ai!" Like lightning, the cane flashes down
on his arm, swings sideways—*whack*—slamming into
his side.

"Ooompf." Matt coughs, rubs his ribs.

"You going to let a girl beat you?" shouts Findley.

Tense, Matt wipes his nose, then starts bouncing on
his toes like he's in a boxing ring. Dashing forward and
back. Hopping left, then right. Feigning a punch. He
squeals, snorts like an angry pig, trying to scare her.

Kiko's sword-cane shifts, aiming at Matt's chest. "I
don't want to hurt you. Let Hip-Hop go."

Matt shrieks, fists flailing. Kiko counters, inching back, left, then right. Matt keeps trying to hit. Though he's taller, stronger, Kiko's thrusts, deflections, easily keep him at bay.

"Come on, Matt. You aren't a loser, are you?" gripes Findley.

Sweating, face flushed, Matt feints left, then right, and tries an uppercut. Kiko knocks his hands away and spins, swinging the cane, adding her body's force. The cane smacks, hard.

Matt gasps, drops to his knees. He's not unconscious, but it's still a knockout. Holding his ribs, moaning, he doesn't want another round.

Kiko hasn't broken a sweat. "Fair and square," she says, then stares at Findley. "You want me to fight you, too?"

"Try it." Findley holds the bag high, higher, above his head.

"Don't drop him, don't drop him," I plead.

"Zane? Zane! Ready, Zane?" Signaling, Kiko cocks her head toward Findley.

Exhaling, bellowing *"Kiai,"* she whacks Findley's arm. Quick, half circling the cane, she strikes upward.

Findley screams; his grip unclenches.

Hip-Hop falls.

I dive, catching Hip-Hop before he crashes. I untie

the bag. "Hip-Hop!" I hug him tight, nearly bursting into tears. "Hip-Hop, Hip-Hop." He licks my cheek. Over and over.

"More?" asks Kiko, aiming the cane unwaveringly. Matt staggers, holding his side. Findley, furious, glares at Kiko.

"Can I pet him?" The sunglass bandanna kid squats. Matt and Findley scold. "Traitor. Sniveling baby."

Up close, from his stubby fingers, it's clear he's a little kid. Eight, maybe?

Gently, awed, the boy strokes Hip-Hop. Like he's patting a dog for the first time.

Captain Maddie?

I turn my head. No one's behind me. I peer again at the boy's glasses. *Reflected in them is Captain Maddie smiling, happier than I've ever seen her.*

"Petey!" yells Findley, tugging his collar. "Get up. Sucking up to the enemy! Wait till I tell Rattler."

Petey cringes.

"Real pirates," Kiko shoots, sarcastic, "don't terrorize boys!"

"What do you know?" snarls Findley, shoving Petey. "Next time, Rattler will take what's ours. You'll wish you paid the ransom."

"Rattler's a coward, if he sent you," I say.

Matt raises his hand to strike.

My back contracts, protecting Hip-Hop.

"Try it," Kiko taunts.

"Come on, Matt." Findley pushes Petey again.

Watching Petey stumble forward, I feel sorry for him. His pants are too big. His tousled hair dirty, matted.

"What's his name?" asks Petey, sneaking a look back.

"Hip-Hop."

Findley pushes Petey again. (Pirates *are* bullies.)

All three lay down their boards, sailing, retreating into the wind.

I stand, holding Hip-Hop. Kiko kisses his head.

"You rocked it, Kiko. Captain Maddie would be so proud of you. I'm proud of you."

She grins.

"Your dad would be proud, too."

"You think so?"

"I know so."

20

Where'd You Go?

"Zane-boy? Where are you? Zane?" John calls.

"Captain John, late, useless again," grumbles Kiko.

"Ahoy, mates. Ahoy!" Captain John, his striped bell-bottoms flaring, gold chains swinging, hurries across the grass.

"Where was he?"

Where? I wonder, burying my nose in Hip-Hop's fur.

"How come you always arrive late?" Kiko demands.

"John, why'd you leave Hip-Hop?"

"Zane, what's wrong with Hip-Hop?"

"Nothing, but not because of you!" gripes Kiko.

"They captured him for ransom, John. The pirate boys."

"No!" Captain John looks stricken. He reaches for Hip-Hop.

Hip-Hop dodges.

"Even Hip-Hop is mad at you," I say.

"Nothing a little jerky can't cure." John offers a piece; Hip-Hop gobbles it.

"See, forgiveness among friends," proclaims John, his hands sweeping dramatically. "A captain cares about the greater good. I was doing reconnaissance."

"It doesn't matter. Me and Kiko are going back to Rockaway."

"You can't," demands John fiercely.

"You're not his dad," snaps Kiko.

John looks stricken. "Of course not! But why, Zane? You're so close."

"Hip-Hop could've been killed. Twice, he almost died. No treasure's worth losing Hip-Hop."

"Courage, Zane. Hopelessness is part of every journey. Every hunt."

"I don't want to listen to you anymore."

"Then don't listen. Feel my words with your heart." John steps back, giving himself more scope. He paces, his hands flailing, conjuring a scene. "Imagine the wide, wild, churning sea. Imagine hurricanes. Thunderstorms. Imagine days and nights of no wind. Your ship dead in the water. Its sails lifeless, limp."

He spins, facing me. "Captain Maddie endured such hardships."

My ears perk.

"Mind you, an adventure without difficulty isn't worth

having. The hunt is harder but the discovery sweeter. Think of Captain Maddie," he appeals. "Think of your mother. Your father." Eyes aglow, his face presses closer, closer to mine. "Think of you."

"What's that mean?" demands Kiko.

"Think of yourself. Nothing worse than a boy who's meant to be a hero disappointing himself."

"What?"

"Not everyone is meant to finish the journey. A captain recognizes when someone else is best suited for uncovering the prize."

John's mesmerizing. The scar on his chin, his peering amber eyes, his snake ring make him seem mysterious, dangerous. (A crew would follow him anywhere.)

Then, soft, ever so softly: "Do you want to remember yourself as a gutless swine?"

"Hey," admonishes Kiko.

"A hero with no heart?"

So close, I see his stubble. Smell his stale breath.

"An explorer afraid of adventure?" His voice rises. "A treasure hunter quitting on the edge of discovery, success? A son disappointing his elders?"

Each question hits me hard. I feel nauseous, disoriented. Since the hunt began, I've been seeing oddities. Ghosts, spirits. A past that isn't past. Even John's voice conjures visions.

(What's real? Concrete? One, true thing?)

"Did Captain Maddie have a son?"

Wary, John straightens, towering over me again. He blocks the green view—trees, bushes, grasses.

I squeeze Hip-Hop.

"Yes."

"What?" I look up.

"Yes. We had a son."

I feel slapped.

"You and Captain Maddie?" gasps Kiko.

John grips my shoulder. "I told you we were best mates. Come to your senses, Zane," he insists, sounding more irritated. "Captain Maddie picked you for a reason. You're her boy, her first mate."

"My head hurts."

Kiko cradles Hip-Hop. "Let's go home, Zane."

"Underground," insists John. "We must go underground."

"What're you talking about?" gripes Kiko.

"Sail the turbulent seas. While you were up in the sky, I went back to the burial ground. Coffins pushed deeper and deeper into the ground. Above, skyscrapers. Beneath, subways. We'll search there, Zane. We'll search there."

"Sure, that's makes sense," says Kiko scornfully, "blow up the subways."

"That's right, Miss Kiko. Blow them up!"

He roams, stomps in the grass. Park visitors steer clear. With each word, he seems to grow bigger, more enthusiastic, like a carny barker. No, a ringmaster enticing me.

"Can't destroy buildings but beneath them, there're miles of dirt tunnels. A whole nether world. My world.

"Sail, Zane. Do you want to go sailing? Bring your board. Hundreds of tunnels, half-completed. A turbulent, underground sea."

"That's what Captain Maddie said, 'turbulent, underground, sea,'" I shout, but I don't think John hears me.

He's obsessed, his locs swaying as he circles, kicking up grass, jabbering obsessively about a fantastical world.

"Tunnels like tributaries," "Broken masts," I hear. "Incomplete rails," "Horizons to explore," "Man the cannons," "Wealth to rival Blackbeard's.

"I knew you'd lead me to the treasure. Come along. Set sail." He strides through the park, past the fountain, heading to who knows where.

"He's nuts, Zane."

Clamoring, he belts staccato: "Ahoy, mate," "Hunt," "Nearly there," "Captain Maddie, let's board."

I can't help but follow. Hip-Hop follows me. Across the park, dodging behind John as he crosses the street, against the stoplight. Brakes screech; horns honk. "To think—treasure right above me and I didn't see. Follow, follow. Follow me, Zane-boy."

Kiko races to keep up. "He's lost his mind."

Muttering, thrashing his hands, John turns right on the sidewalk. People part around him, avoiding the wild man. Listing down Broadway, he passes City Hall station, the Woolworth Building.

Kiko clasps my arm. "Don't, Zane. Let's go home."

I hesitate. *Steer true.* Captain Maddie shouldn't have died. "I've come too far, Kiko. I've got to follow him," I say, my heart pounding.

John's jubilant, moving faster.

"We should just end this, Zane," she yells. "Go home to Rockaway. I'll ask my dad to give your mom the money. To pay the back taxes."

Abruptly, I stop. "Don't Kiko. Just don't." I unstrap my board, swerving, then leaping off the curb into the bike lane.

"It's impossible. You'll never find the treasure," she screams.

I kick my leg and sail, focusing on John's bobbing head, the flash of his striped bell-bottoms moving along the packed street. He's headed for a subway staircase.

"This is our last chance," I say, glancing at Hip-Hop, running alongside. "Treasure. I've got to believe.

"Sail, Hip-Hop. We're going to be rich," I howl. "Rich."

CHAMBERS STREET STATION

John descends, bellowing, "My ship, my ship." Singing, "Safe and sound at home again, let the waters roar. Faldee raldee raldee raldee rye-eye-doe."

My spirits lift. Following John, I know I'll save the day. Save our home.

I leap off the skateboard, rush down concrete steps.

At the top of the stairs, Kiko cries, "I won't follow you, Zane. I *won't*."

Two paws at a time, Hip-Hop hops, following me. Going down, down the steps into a ceramic-tiled concrete ocean of people, strident voices, squealing and whistling trains.

Subway Underground

A transit guard in a white shirt and orange vest stands by the turnstile. I don't have any money. *Flash, distract.*

"Full sail ahead." Hip-Hop and my board zoom beneath the turnstile. My right hand leverages my body up and over.

"Hey, no dogs! Pay the fare!"

Before the guard can stop me, Kiko jumps over the turnstile, too, landing coolly on her board. Dope and smooth.

"You came?"

Kiko nods, adjusting her backpack. "Wouldn't miss it."

"Right. What're friends for?" I quip.

Like magic, Captain John appears. "The kids are okay." He swipes a MetroCard.

"Only service dogs allowed."

"He is a service dog." John puffs out his chest. "I swiped for him, too."

The guard scowls.

Hip-Hop lifts his paw.

"Problem?" asks John, threatening.

"No," says the much smaller man, shaking his head.

"Let's go, Miss Kiko. Zane-boy."

"Where're we going?"

The platform is crowded with commuters, some sitting, some leaning against concrete poles. Overhead, electric lights *bzzzz-bzzzz.* Some flickering. Some casting too-white, ghostly light. Graffiti covers the walls.

On the far track, a train rumbles, screeches. Opens, closes doors. Wheels turn, slow, picking up speed, faster, faster until the train disappears.

Intense, John turns to us. "Six minutes, that's all we've got. Run, fast as you can, down the track. Got to make it to the service alcove."

"Or what?" asks Kiko.

"Pinned. Smashed against the wall."

John darts through the crowd, leaps onto the gritty tracks.

I follow. "Jump, Hip-Hop." He jumps into my arms.

Lining the platform edge, people are wailing, screaming.

Kiko's frozen, fearful, staring at the electrified rails.

"Hurry," bellows John, barely visible in the dark tunnel.

"You don't have to come, Kiko."

She looks at me. I can tell she wants to say, "No."
"Stop." "Don't go!" Then she closes her eyes. Inhales.
Her features smooth, her eyes open.

"I'm coming." She's warrior girl, focused, intense. She
scrambles down. "Let's go!"

We race, knowing our lives depend upon it.

Darkness is smothering, blinding. Heat and a greasy,
rotting-animal smell gags me. I run.

John's arm reaches, grabbing me. "Here."

Startled, I cry out, and quickly spin, calling, "Kiko!"

Me and John are in a small alcove, an elevated,
cutout space in the tunnel wall.

I squint. Kiko's still running. Maybe a minute behind.

Tracks squeal. Headlights shine. The eastbound
train rattles the walls, barreling faster and faster
down the rails, closer and closer.

"Kiko! Run."

She's gasping.

I reach down.

She tries to clasp my hand, but sweat makes our
palms slip.

"You can make it! You've gotta make it."

Like a halo, light illuminates from behind her.
Headlights are so close; the halo glows wider. Bigger.

Grunting, arm outstretched, she leaps. Our hands
connect!

Tight, ever so tight, both my hands hold her hand. John grips her waist, pulling her up into the alcove seconds before the train roars by. One second, two seconds, five . . . ten. A long line of metal subway cars rumble, exploding air. Twelve seconds, thirteen, fourteen. . . . The noise is unbearable.

Cramped into a concrete alcove, we hold on to each other. Hip-Hop leans against my legs.

Eighteen, nineteen, twenty seconds. Scared, holding our breath, hearts pounding, me and Kiko shudder.

Gone. One last gust of wind. Sparks fly, and the subway zooms, the harsh, metallic *clackety-clack, clickety-clack* receding.

Relieved, I sigh.

John laughs. "Excitement, brave mates!"

Spinning a padlock right, then left, then right again, he unlocks a thick chain, pushes open a steel door. "Welcome to my world." He claps loudly twice. An array of lights—red, blue, green, white—zigzag like ship's rigging across the wide abandoned tunnel's roof.

The rest is a huge, circular, seemingly infinite, hole. Nothing but darkness at the far end. The sides are concave concrete—like a skate bowl but wide enough to ride a subway train through.

"This is amazing." As I speak, the sound of *whizzzzing* skateboard wheels, more frightening than trains, grows louder and louder.

The pirate crew! First, the bandanna kid. Petey! Then the boys arrive in twos—Matt and Findley. All dressed in black, grungy clothes with snaps, zippers, torn leggings. They skate fast, sharp, taunting us with skill and attitude. Making circle eights, flybys in front and in back of us. S swerves.

Me and Kiko don't move. Hip-Hop growls, baring his teeth.

Still facing us, John walks backward.

Rattler skates circling him, then depressing his board's tail, stops. Stands tall beside John.

One kid with a skull and crossbones on his shirt does a powerslide against the wall. Others jump, popping their boards up into their hands, exposing skull-and-bones undersides. Some tail drag or heel scrape.

Over a dozen skaters now. Four carry torches, flaming yellow-red with black spiraling smoke.

One last skater, whizzing fast, head down, does a difficult bluntside. His board slides ninety degrees; his heel drags.

He halts beside Rattler, then lifts his head.

"Jack!" me and Kiko shout, bolting forward.

Menacing, John thrusts out a flattened palm.

We stop.

John's face is ugly, twisted. No wide, grinning smile. No swaying, hand-waving barker. Just a big, solid, unsmiling man, daring us to pass.

"Jack, what's this mean? What's going on?"

Jack acts like he doesn't recognize me. Rattler, I think, wishes his eyes could slay. He pounds his fist into his palm. The other skaters look scornful, mean. Their shadows stretch thin and tall, arcing up the tunnel's circular side.

Despairing, I sigh.

A solid, unbeatable crew against two skaters and a dog.

"Zane-boy," says John with no trace of an accent, "you've steered well. Solved the clues. Now it's time for Captain John to be in charge.

"This is my crew. You've met Rattler, my first mate."

Rattler preens, turning, flapping his hands as the boys applaud and cheer.

"I'll be taking the treasure for me and my crew."

"No, John," I shout, dismayed. "You planned to betray us—*me*—all along?"

"Pirates pirate," answers John. "Attack and rob."

I stagger back.

"It's pirate nature, Zane-boy. You can't expect me to be other than I am."

But I did. *Stupid, stupid, stupid.*

Grown-ups aren't supposed to betray kids. My stomach clenches, my hands tremble. There were warning signs. I ignored them.

John towers over me, serious, stern.

Fool.

"Jack's already joined us. So, he'll get a share of the treasure."

"Is this true?"

Jack won't look at me.

"How about you, Zane-boy?" John grins, trying to be persuasive. "Join us and get a share."

I shake my head, jeering, "I believed you. Kiko was right all along. You're a thief and a liar!"

Captured

"Come on, Kiko. Let's get out of here."

"Oh, no, I can't let you go. Not until we find the treasure, Zane-boy. I can't risk you calling the police. Stop them, mates!" orders John.

The crew yell, hoot, scream war cries. In a flash, they sail, surrounding us.

No escape. Nowhere to run or skate.

Taunting, Rattler faces me as two pirates pin my arms beneath my back, roping my hands together. I look at Jack, my eyes pleading. *Help me.*

He glances away.

Kiko, centered, knees bent, grips one strap of her backpack as a pirate tugs the other. "Give it over," he yells.

"Just grab the cane," howls John. "The treasure map's inside."

The boy jerks the handle and triumphantly snatches the cane.

Defeated, Kiko drops the backpack.

Quick, Matt and Findley grip her, tie her hands.

Hip-Hop crawls into the pack. Petey reaches for it. Hip-Hop snarls, jaw jutting. The kid tries again. Ferocious, Hip-Hop snaps. But he doesn't break skin.

"Oww," whines Petey, dejected, sucking his bruised hand. (I feel sorry for him.)

Matt smacks him.

Petey droops.

"Leave the backpack," yells John. "We've got the map. Back to the harbor, mates! Bring the prisoners along."

"Move," says Rattler snidely, forcing me onward. "Worst first mate ever! Loser. Failure."

Rattler's words sting. I *am* a failure. I should've listened to Kiko. From the beginning, Petey, then Matt and Findley, were tracking me. Making it easy for John to show up as a helper, a rescuer. Find me at the African Burial Ground Monument.

Hard, Rattler shoves between my shoulders. I stumble.

Kiko exclaims, "Not fair." Then, more loudly, "That means you, too, Jack! Not fair to abandon us. Traitor."

I feel punched in the gut. I thought I could always count on Jack.

Moving forward, looking back, I holler, "Come on, Hip-Hop."

He doesn't move. Just lies, defensive in Kiko's backpack. His beady brown eyes watch me.

He's trying to tell me something. (Dogs should be able to talk.)

Hip-Hop growls, his teeth bared.

Fair, I think. Hip-Hop's smarter than me. Unlike me, he's figured out how to keep himself safe.

Unlike me, he doesn't surrender to pirates.

Harbor

We all trudge a mile. Mainly, I think, because John isn't on a skateboard.

From time to time, boys slam their skateboards down, dash off, race each other, then double back to walk some more. Some jostle, elbow each other. Some even slap, punch. Petey is teased the most. A curly-headed boy shoves him off his board. Another kid, a skull-and-crossbones tattoo on his neck, steals it, then skates off as Petey, the bandanna kid, chases.

"Can't catch me!" the thief teases.

Jack skates to him, speaks. I can't hear what he's saying; he's too far off to the side. But whatever he says makes the tattooed kid hand him the board.

Jack skates and gives the board back to Petey.

I'm glad. Jack never did like bullying. (But why's he here?)

Rattler leaves my side. Skates to Jack. Twisting my

head, I try to keep track of them as me and Kiko and the crew pass.

I think Jack and Rattler are arguing. Both are frowning, chests poked out, standing toe-to-toe. For the first time, I think of how often Jack had to protect himself from his dad. Rattler doesn't scare him.

But, if I'm truthful, Rattler scares me.

I'm confused, thirsty. Hungry. My throat aches.

I feel small, walking through the gargantuan concrete tubes. About every quarter mile, there's another tunnel that juts off to the right or left. But not all the tunnels seem finished. Some are just dirt rounds, braced with beams.

How long has it been like this? An abandoned, underground world. No, that's not right—not abandoned. Captain John and his crew claimed it.

"Home, mates. Back to port!" John proclaims, arms wide, moving in spiraling circles, showing off his docked ship. More rows, strings of twinkling Christmas lights. Skull-and-crossbones flags hang from masts and the rounded ceiling.

Bunk-bed structures are on the left and right. But instead of bunk beds, there are tied hammocks. An upper deck and lower deck of woven rope.

Four trash cans and a dumpster are grouped, burning wood. Kids, some smaller, younger than Petey, roast chickens on spits. (Where'd these little kids come from? Why aren't they home?)

Kiko looks queasy.

"You okay?" I whisper.

"I'll make it," she whispers, smiling weakly.

The tunnel feels claustrophobic. No fresh air. Trash-barrel grilled chicken is the worst. Nauseating.

I slouch. It's my fault Kiko's here. Never once did she say, "Told you so."

"So sorry, Kiko."

She bumps her shoulder against mine.

John sits in a leather reclining chair. Feet up, his back inclined, he surveys us, his crew. Four poles wrapped in white twinkling lights square a deck. Beams are draped with cotton sails.

Rattler shoves us forward. I search for Jack. No sign.

"You should make them kneel," says Rattler.

Older boys chant, hoot, "Kneel, kneel, kneel." Some spin skateboard wheels; others drum their boards. The noise is deafening.

"I'm a captain, mind you. Not a king." John chuckles, basking in their acclaim.

I glare angrily. Mad at myself for being duped.

"Untie us," demands Kiko.

"Gladly. Once you swear loyalty to me."

"Are you kidding?"

"Never," I say.

"Zane-boy, you disappoint me. Admit you're a reluctant mutineer. You felt a bond with me. Don't deny it."

"I trusted you."

"I know. I feel guilty for deceiving you. Such a loyal, trusting boy. Now, Miss Kiko," he says, slamming his feet to the ground, "was a mutineer from the start. Always doubting. Even at her most annoying, I admire her. So very, very smart."

"You're not the heroic pirate from the 'olden days,' are you, John?" Kiko snaps back. "You're a thug. A crook."

John bolts upright. The charming, smiling barker replaced by a ruthless, fierce-eyed pirate.

He doesn't scare me.

"I've got a soft spot for you, Zane-boy. But not you, Miss Kiko." He walks closer. Places his hand on my shoulder.

I flinch.

"Zane is trusting and naive. Like I was as a boy."

"He's a mutineer. They both should walk the plank!" crows Rattler.

Shouts reverberate: "Walk the plank, walk the plank."

I slip my shoulder out from beneath John's hand. He looks hurt.

"Walk the plank!" Rattler urges. The chant grows louder. "Walk the plank, walk the plank!"

"No," booms John. He stoops, leans in, whispering, "Zane-boy, join me. I can be a father to you."

I shut my eyes against his gaze. Loss, loneliness constrict my throat.

John's mouth hovers near my ear. "Stay with me and your best friend, Jack."

"I won't, I won't!"

John recoils. "Think it over, Zane-boy. I'm being kind. One night to think it over. Jack," he calls.

Seemingly out of nowhere, Jack appears.

"Escort Zane and Kiko to my room."

"Follow me," says Jack, shielding, shoving against the screaming, wild, flailing boys pushing to get close. "Hurry."

Jack shifts left. Another tunnel. But after six feet, cloth hanging from a line makes a back wall.

Once inside, Jack slides the front cloth, closing us in. Furnishings are sparse. A cot, blankets, floor pillows. A small table with a metal cup.

We still hear chants: "Walk the plank! Walk the plank."

John orders, "Quiet. Do as you're told! Tomorrow, we sail the underground sea for centuries-lost gold."

Voices yell, "Hurrah." A few holler, "Walk the plank."

A loud clap. Then a chilling bellow: "Disobey me, at your peril!"

Silence. Eerie silence. As if everyone had disappeared. Beyond the curtain, it's a ghost ship.

"I'll bring food. Water," says Jack.

"Why, Jack?" I ask.

"Yes, why?"

Sad-eyed, he murmurs, "I'm different than you two."

I press, "Different, how?"

"No family."

"You've got a family."

"Really, Kiko? Coming from you?"

"Sorry about your dad."

"Can't fault you for the truth, Kiko. He hates me."

"What about your mom?"

Jack inhales, steadies himself. "She doesn't defend
me. Never did. Even when I was little, she said, 'A boy
needs to learn how to defend himself.' When Dad starts
whaling on me, she leaves the mobile home."

Straining against her tied hands, Kiko cries quietly,
her cheek against Jack's chest. "I'm so sorry."

Jack was always the brave one. I counted on his
strength.

Jack hugs Kiko. "Don't be sad. Lately, I've been
landing a few good punches."

Not enough, I think. Jack's dad is big, muscular like
a tank. (Uneven odds. Not fair.)

"You didn't have to leave us, Jack." My voice trembles. "You've always been with me. Me, with you. Friends." Embarrassed, I look away.

"Listen," he replies hurriedly. "Help John find the treasure, then he'll let you go. You'll be safer."

"Why stay? Here? Underground?"

"Here, everyone's a throwaway. Or a runaway. John gives us a home. Pirates who live, eat, sleep—"

"Steal?"

"Yes, Kiko, steal together. After we escaped the Oyster House, John explained he looks out for lost boys who'd otherwise be starved, jailed, or in foster care. Stealing from those who already have enough isn't wrong."

"Who're you to decide, Jack? John's stealing my chance to save me and Ma's home."

Jack's face is unreadable. He tugs the ends of Kiko's hair. "I wasn't really mad at you. Just mad at how unfair life is. Wish I had your dad, Dr. Kitaji. Or"—he looks at me—"no dad."

"Don't say that. John's worse. He doesn't care about anyone. He caused Captain Maddie's death."

"If you'd lived my life, Zane, you'd know sometimes people get hurt."

"No," Kiko sobs.

I'm stunned. I didn't realize how bitter Jack is. Sometimes I'd skate, walk him home. His mom always seemed distracted, nice. She'd wave from the front

door. But when his dad was home, off the road, he'd
insist I stay away.

"I should've done more to help."

Lopsided, Jack's mouth twists. "No guilt, Zane.
Adults should've helped."

"And you think John's helping?"

"Yes," he answers gravely. "Here, I'll survive. Help
the youngest boys."

"Like Petey?"

Jack's eyes dull. "Older kids bully the youngest.
It isn't fair. As I grew, my dad had to work harder to
scare, intimidate me.

"When you're little, you don't realize it'll get better.
You forget what it's like to have someone look out for
you."

Always, Jack looked out for me. Me, him. Not anymore.

Lifting a brow, Jack asks, "Where's rat dog?"

I can't speak.

Jack nods. Seems to know I'm heartbroken.

He lifts the curtain and, without turning or looking
at us, warns, "Watch out for Rattler." He leaves.

Kiko cries. Big, gurgling, sobs.

John's cot has a mountain of blankets. Some silk,
some wool. Using my feet, I kick, drag some of the
blankets onto the floor. Awkward, bending our knees,
we collapse.

Kiko quiets, whimpers, rests her head in my lap.

I swallow tears. I didn't know I could feel this bad. Such a dingy, hopeless journey. Nothing but loss. Captain Maddie. Hip-Hop. Now Jack.

Kiko's asleep. The warmth, weight of her head are comforting. I don't want to lose her, too.

Holding my breath, I strain, listening for Hip-Hop.

Two days ago, we were sneaking down the steps of my home. Hip-Hop's nails scratching *clickity-clack*. Now I'm on my own.

Will he want to find me? Be my best dog again?

Blow the Man Down

"Blow, blow, blow the man down," John sings. He's jovial in his bell-bottom pants with a red scarf tied about his head.

Captain Flint clings to his shoulder.

Voices echo back, "Blow, blow, blow the man down. Way, hey, blow the man down."

John and his sailors sing, "Give me some time to blow the man down!"

"A bonny good mate and a captain, too," John sings alone. "A bonny good ship and a bonny good crew. Way, hey, blow the man down."

"Playacting," says Kiko. "Stupid playacting."

"Way, hey, blow the man down," the boys reply. "Blow, blow, blow the man down."

Some walk, some skate, others carry boxes, drag shovels and burlap stuffed with gunpowder sticks. They're all following John. A riotous parade. Some hold torches; others, flashlights. A few boards are lit with mini headlights.

"Unhinged," I say. "John thinks he's going to find the treasure."

"Shut your trap," commands Rattler.

Kiko rolls her eyes.

I tug my bound hands, wishing I could punch Rattler. Punch my way home.

Tunnels are everywhere—north to south, east to west. The tunnel we're in hasn't been covered in concrete. There aren't any hanging lights. Instead, Petey and three others carry torches. Underground—it *is* like a separate sea. There's no way of knowing what it's like topside—is it sunny, raining? Cloudless or cloudy skies? Funny, people are going about their business not knowing about unfinished subway trails and hollowed-out dirt.

Hand high, Captain John stops. The torch bearers draw closer, casting light and shadows across his face.

Captain Flint squawks, "Pieces of eight."

"Now, mates," John says, unexpectedly somber, "we're going to blow up dirt, dig for treasure. Zane-boy, our mutineer, figured out the clues." He slaps me on the back, weaving between his crew. Touching a boy's shoulder here and there. Staring, smiling at others, ruffling Petey's hair.

"Long ago—or should I say 'once upon a time'?—pirate brothers transported runaway slaves and a chest of jewels and gold meant to fund the underground railroad. Now, pirates being pirates," grinning, John beckons, "they delivered the black gold but wanted to keep the gold gold."

Boisterous, the mates cheer.

"Where's the honor, John?" I shout. "The pirate loyalty?"

"Shut up," says Rattler.

"Mind you, Zane-boy, pirate loyalty is only meant for pirates. If pirates don't trust each other, how else are they to live, sail through bad, hard times?"

"What about only stealing from the rich?" Kiko shouts.

"Ah, abolitionists were rich. Northern, softhearted widows, guilt-ridden leaders, and bleeding-heart churchgoers. Folks who wouldn't stop funding abolition if a treasure chest or two were lost.

"Thomas Downing was a millionaire. He didn't need the money. He hid the chest in the Black cemetery. Where it's lain for over two hundred years. Who would ever think to look for gold with bones?"

"You," calls Rattler.

"Yes, me. Fulfilling a captain's quest for his mates."

"Didn't you say Zane solved the clues?"

Everyone stares, astonished by Jack's outburst.

Rattler snarls, "Don't disrespect the code. Truth is what the captain says it is."

Tension stretches between Jack and Rattler.

"Now, mates," says John, being expansive, "today is a good day. I, no one else, am finishing the journey. You're my trusty crew."

Boys hoot, holler.

"We're searching for X marks the spot. It may take days or a month, mind you, but we'll find treasure."

Skaters cheer, chant, "Captain John, Captain John."

Again, he raises his hand for quiet. "Treasure was buried, not below us, but above. Over six acres that rich New Yorkers built atop graves.

"Some graves have been discovered. But not the treasure!"

"So, what're we going to do?" asks Petey.

"Bomb! Dig dirt."

"So stupid," Kiko adds.

"Bring the gunpowder." Burlap bags are placed before John. "Inch by inch, mile by mile, tunnel by tunnel," he says, voice rising, "we'll clear from below the old cemetery ground.

"Findley, Petey, Devon, and Jace—place the tubes of gunpowder as high as possible."

Petey and Jace are slight, smaller. (Cabin boys?)

Deftly, like an acrobat, Jace jumps, and Devon lifts

him onto his shoulders. He grips Jace's legs, steadying him.

Petey, clumsier, sways, high atop Findley. He clutches Findley's head.

"Be calm, Petey," yells Rattler.

Findley offers gunpowder sticks.

"Unbelievable," I cry. "Dangerous. Jack, tell them! They'll get hurt."

"If you want to go free, Zane-boy," warns John, "keep your trap shut."

Rattler punches my stomach. Coughing, I double over.

Gunpowder coils with wicks are driven into the tunnel's sides, its unfinished ceiling. Alternating left side, right side, Petey and Jace don't cluster the sticks too close. Still, I worry about a cave-in.

"Fire away," John orders.

Another boy hands Petey a torch. He lights the wick, leaps off Findley's shoulders. Both race toward me, Kiko, and Jack. We huddle against the earth wall.

Boom. A shower of dirt, rock, pebbles. A jagged gape lies between the wall and rounded ceiling.

"Dig, boys."

Several of the taller boys lift shovels, jabbing at the hole. More dirt cascades; the boys shield their eyes.

"Dig."

Shovels scrape, twist at the packed dirt. As more earth loosens, shovels keep digging, upward and out.

"More light!"

Others crowd around John, beneath the hole and showering dirt.

John yells, "Nothing! No treasure. Blow another stick. Two sticks."

Rattler dashes forward, leaps up, torches two gunpowder sticks on the right wall.

"Everyone back," shouts Jack. "Watch out."

Kiko screams.

I stoop, frustrated I can't shield my head. Frustrated that Rattler thinks he's so cool.

Boom. Boom. Chunks of the ceiling drop. Huge mounds of heavy dirt, amid showering rocks.

John jumps back. "Close call."

Some boys shudder; others laugh nervously.

"Come on," shouts John, commanding. "Dig."

Mates rush forward. They use the shovels' points to chip away, destroy the tunnel's shape. Rattler stands on a box, shoveling almost horizontal. He grunts, attacking the top wall.

"That's my first mate," shouts John. Rattler jams the shovel deeper, twisting it, pushing it deeper. An earth slide, a thunderous waterfall of dirt. Rattler tips over, falls. Others run. Scream.

John scrapes at the dirt pile covering Rattler. "You all right? Rattler?"

Gasping, face smeared, shedding dirt, Rattler sits up, triumphantly holding a bone.

"Remarkable," breathes John, dropping to his knees. "Skeletons and treasure, side by side."

Like ants, the crew digs uncovering pieces of the dead and disintegrating wood.

Singing off-key, Findley pretends a bone is a microphone. "Blow, blow, blow the man down." Devon and Jace fence with two larger bones (a leg? an arm bone?).

Emphatic, Kiko says, "Show some respect."

(No one pays her any attention.)

Captain John jams the shovel farther into the wall. He crows as more bones are uncovered. Sticking out of the packed dirt. Two-fisted, he plucks them, then drops them to the floor. "Only a matter of time before we're all rich." He tugs, tearing a rotting coffin from the wall.

"How can you stand him?" I ask Jack as we three hang back, huddled in the shadows.

"You defended him, too, Zane. Remember?"

"I shouldn't have."

"Too late." Kiko rolls her eyes again.

"He's not so bad."

"How can you say that?"

Jack sighs. "Better a pirate than being neglected."

"Ridiculous," snorts Kiko.

"No, I get it," I respond bitterly. "What boy doesn't want to be a pirate?"

"Light the rest!" calls John. "All the powder! Boom, boom, boom!"

"Too much," I call, running to John. Hands bound, I wish I could shake him. Pull him and the others away. "It's too dangerous."

"What a good-hearted kid you are, Zane-boy," answers John, clapping my back. "Your father raised you proper.

"But this is a battle. Pirates explode cannons. Isn't that right, mates?" He twirls slowly, fingers wriggling, arms wide, as if he were embracing everyone.

The boys are mesmerized. Jaws slack, eyes wide. "Admiration," like Jack said. *Worship?* A room filled with hungry expressions. Awe. A mood of glittering, gleamy giddiness.

Who doesn't want to be a pirate? Derring-do, adventure. Treasure. Family loyalty. Above all, loyalty to John.

"Jack, do something; say something."

He shrugs. (I don't think I ever knew him.)

With Petey's sunglasses off, I can see his fear. Petey's squirming, nervous. Again, he climbs Findley's back, swings his legs over his shoulders.

Findley hands Petey a fierce, flaming torch.

"Not enough time," I scream.

The wicks are long, but safely lighting three sticks spaced six feet apart seems impossible.

Findley moves to the farthest stick. Petey lights. Findley jogs forward.

"Run," I call. But it isn't easy carrying a kid.

Petey sweeps the torch. The wick doesn't light.

"Wait," he screeches, trying again. "Okay, go!"

The third wick hisses, burning.

Boom. Dirt crashes, sounding like the world is tearing itself apart.

Boom. The second stick. A chunk of wall disintegrates.

"Run," I cry. "Run."

Boom.

Findley stumbles. Thick, hard dirt traps his legs. Petey tumbles. The torch arcs, twirls like a giant sparkler, landing on Petey's back.

"Help him, Jack," I yell, rattled, frustrated my hands are tied.

Jack's on it. Kicking aside the torch, he drops, patting Petey's shirt, smothering flames. "It's okay," he murmurs. "You're going to be okay."

"That's right," says John, standing over them. "A badge of honor."

"Unbelievable," shouts Kiko.

Petey groans. Beneath his shirt's jagged burnouts, his skin is red, blistering.

"Seen ship gunpowder wounds many a time. He'll be fine, Miss Kiko. Just as I told you that Zane-boy would be fine after falling overboard."

"He's got second-degree burns. Who's got water? We need to cool his skin. Untie me, Jack," she demands.

"Me too."

Jack looks to John, urging, "They can help get Petey back to camp. We'll take care of him. The rest of you"—he glances at the shocked, scared pirates—"can treasure hunt." He raises his voice louder, falsely jovial. "We'll fix Petey, right as rain! Promise. A little rest and he'll rejoin his mates!"

All, except for Rattler and John, cheer.

Lips pressed tight, John nods. "Come on, boys," he orders, "let's hunt." Then he clutches Jack's shirt. "Don't let them get away."

"You'll be sorry if they do," adds Rattler, grinning at the thought.

Pulling a knife from his jeans, Jack cuts our ties.

Kiko rips Petey's shirt. Devon hands her a canteen. She pours water onto the cloth, gently patting, cooling Petey's skin. Stopping the burn.

"That's as much as I can do," she says. "We need pain ointment. Antibiotics."

"I'll carry him," says Jack.

Petey screams as he's lifted. His hands flail, smacking

Jack's face and arms. Finally, he gasps, shudders, and falls limp.

"He's fainted," says Kiko. "Hurry."

Gripping Petey in a fireman's carry, Jack jogs beside her. (I'd forgotten how strong he is.)

"When you tire, Jack, I'll help."

He doesn't hear me. He and Kiko dart left into an east-west tunnel, retracing our steps.

I can't help it. I look back.

John, with Rattler by his side, furiously digs, searches.

Jace, on Devon's shoulders, places more gunpowder. Findley, dirtier than hurt, carries the extra gunpowder and torch.

Stupid, stupid, stupid.

Others are happily digging. Tossing skeletons like ordinary sticks.

I remember the Sankofa etched in the Wall of Remembrance.

"Look at this." A kid holds a skull and happily throws it to his mate.

My stomach clutches. Bile rises.

What if someone disrespected my father's bones?

I gag, wishing I could pass out. Be like Petey, unconscious. Out of this world.

Burn

Kiko's in EMT mode. Competent, worried. Trying to ease Petey's pain.

From a small medical kit, Jack hands her burn ointment, gauze, and ibuprofen. Her hands work delicately, fast, smoothing on the ointment. "This will help with the pain and healing." She drapes gauze on the scarred skin. "When Petey wakes, we'll give him the ibuprofen. It'll help some."

"Petey's a good kid. He's John's scout. Small, he moves secretive, fast."

"He won't be moving fast for a while."

"It's horrible," I say. "John didn't seem to care if he—or anyone—gets hurt. How old is Petey? Eight? Nine? He should be in school."

"Life's tough." Face hardening, Jack abruptly parts the curtain, leaving us again.

I shake my head. (I thought I knew him.)

Flat on his stomach on the cot, Petey is helpless.

"He's going to be fine," says Kiko, sitting next to me on the floor. "The burns aren't as bad as I thought." Both of us have our arms wrapped about our knees. In the distance, we hear explosions. Earth heaving, trembling. (If they keep at it, caves will collapse.)

A candle flickers, casting eerie, shifting shadows. *Boom, boom.*

I imagine skeletons falling out of the dirt. Piece by piece.

Click-click: bones people. Puzzle it out.

"Kiko, Captain Maddie told me about the dead. 'Bones people,' she called them."

"Hey, look who I found," says Jack, holding a wriggling Hip-Hop under his arm.

"Hip-Hop!" We scramble up, embrace Jack holding Hip-Hop—a loving, sandwich hug. Hip-Hop licks my face.

I cry, not caring if Jack and Kiko see.

"Little dude was carting Kiko's backpack. Strong jaws, right?"

Kiko grabs the strap. "Thank you, Hip-Hop."

The small chest from the Downing's cellar tumbles out, cracks.

"What's this?" Jack puts Hip-Hop down.

I collect the pieces—the wood-carved canoe, the gold coin, the note begging, "Keep the cargos safe."

"Did John see these?"

"No. He was punching, kicking the wall, furious we hadn't found the treasure. He didn't pay me and Kiko any mind.

"But these clues helped me understand the story. Proved pirates transported runaways. Oystermen, Black and Native, secretly rowed them to shore."

"And the coin? The note?"

"Proved there was treasure. You kept it all safe, Hip-Hop! How could I have doubted you?"

He yips, rolls over for a belly rub.

Boom, boom resounds throughout the tunnels. We shudder. Hip-Hop howls.

Jack shakes his head. "Pirates betrayed African Americans?"

"Like John's doing now," I say mournfully. "Disturbing graves—ex-slaves, free people. Their descendants."

"Everybody's done it," says Kiko angrily. "Colonists didn't care about a Black cemetery. For centuries, folks kept building over and through their graves. They didn't even bother to finish the subway. To salvage the bones."

"Full circle. Pirates to pirates," adds Jack.

Boom—another explosion. *Boom.*

Petey moans.

Hip-Hop barks. Then bites the small chest, holding it between teeth, shaking it, quick and strong.

"Hip-Hop, put it down."

"What's the matter with him?" asks Kiko.

"Wait," I say. "Listen."

"Something's rattling."

Hip-Hop drops the chest. I pick it up, shaking, hearing the rattle. I turn it over. Another false bottom? I press hard; the pine wood cracks.

"Wow. Look at this."

A key. Not an ordinary key but an elongated brass key with a curlicue handle.

"A skeleton key."

"Must be almost two hundred years old," says Kiko.

"Or older," replies Jack.

"More proof there's buried treasure," I exclaim. "Hip-Hop, you're a genius!" I cup his narrow face. "You *can* talk, can't you?"

Hip-Hop licks me.

I swear, he smiles.

Walking the Plank

I keep guard while Jack, Kiko, and Hip-Hop sleep. Petey, too. Watching his face, I can tell he's in pain. Locked in some awful place between sleep and wakefulness.

Petey's a kid like me. All the pirate skaters are. John manipulates them. Just like he manipulated me.

This isn't a harbor. It's a dank, stale underground. It's not a home. No bathrooms, refrigerators. Just a foul place for boys.

None of that would matter, maybe, if John loved them.

Occasionally, Petey surfaces. He murmurs, "Ma?" before diving, deep down again, inside himself.

Ma—his mother probably loved him. Misses him.

Ma. I love her. She's my reason for finding the treasure.

But maybe it shouldn't be just about me and Ma? Lots of people are in danger of losing their home. Or already don't have a home, like Petey.

Ma—what if I don't make it back to her? I feel sick.

And Kiko? What if John keeps us both prisoners? Ma and Kiko's parents would grieve. Maybe think we ran away on purpose?

Arms wrapped about my knees, I rock.

Worse, what if the abandoned tunnels collapse? What if John and his crew bury us alive? Would any treasure be worth that?

I swallow a scream.

Whizz-whizzzzz. I flinch. Sailors are port-bound. *Stop thinking like John!* "Pirates" are his lie.

I pull back the curtain.

Dragging their feet, skateboards rolling slow, the boys return, exhausted, filthy.

"What a lazy crew!" John berates, shoving a kid off his board. "Can't find treasure if it was right in front of your noses."

(What a jerk! Do the boys know he has another home? Clean, comfortable.)

"We'll do better next time," calls Rattler, trying to ease John's fury. "Won't we, mates?"

(Rattler must know that John's a hypocrite. He's a hypocrite, too, stirring up the boys.)

"Shut up, Rattler. Shut up, John. You're not pirates. This isn't a ship. Not even a home."

Jack bolts awake. "Stop it, Zane. You don't want to see John angry."

"It's true," screams Kiko, stumbling up, railing

beside me. "Look at you." She points at the boys. "Grave robbers, treating people's bones like sticks."

John rushes forward. "Landlubbers, both! Prideful Miss Kiko. And Zane, a mama's boy. Worse, a weak, whiny boy missing his dad."

I go berserk. Full-on berserk.

I'm hitting, kicking, punching John. Screaming, "You betrayed me."

I fall flat, seeing stars. (John slapped, shoved me, I'm not sure which.)

I'm heartbroken.

"Walk the plank," Rattler yells. "They disrespected the captain! Walk the plank."

"Walk the plank, walk the plank!" The chant cascades, building in power, momentum.

Kiko helps me stand. "I've got you."

"Walk the plank," Rattler sneers.

John's face is expressionless. The boys, reenergized by Rattler, shout, "Walk the plank." They don't seem like kids anymore. Ugly, twisted faces. Fierce, bloodthirsty pirates.

"What say you, Zane-boy? Join me? Join Captain John's pirate crew?"

"Never."

"You're all losers," screams Kiko.

Rattler and Matt drag me and Kiko to a makeshift ladder.

"Leave them alone," demands Jack.

"You can walk the plank, too," warns Rattler. "If they refuse to walk, they'll get a beatdown."

Jack's hands clench, unclench. Younger boys like Jace and a pair of towheaded twins, even a few older boys like Matt, align behind him. (Rattler isn't liked by everyone.)

"It's okay. We've got this, Jack," says Kiko.

(Sure, we've got this.)

A narrow plank like a balance beam crosses beneath the cement ceiling. We're supposed to walk under a fake sky of twinkling lights. High in the air. High enough to be hurt if we fall. Seriously hurt.

Kiko hugs me. "We can do this, Zane."

"Walk the plank, walk the plank."

Devon, grinning, shoves us, forcing us to climb the ladder. Findley, his backup, waves a club.

Each rung, rising higher and higher, puts us in more danger. We make it to the top—a small landing like a crow's nest.

At least twenty feet below, I see Hip-Hop, his paws on the ladder, trying to climb up.

Jack lifts Hip-Hop, cradling and soothing him. I catch his gaze. He nods, encouraging me. (If the worst happens, Jack will care for Hip-Hop.)

Staring upward, arms clasped, John looks grim.

Boys hop, pounding, smacking bones, chanting,

"Walk the plank. Walk the plank." Younger boys, like Jace, build piles of stones. Devon and Findley scavenge skeleton parts.

Kiko steps out first, her foot steady. She wobbles as a bone soars past. "Hey, what the heck?"

"Almost a hit," yells Matt as he readies for another throw. Findley lets a rib bone fly. Others throw rocks.

Kiko wobbles, tries to duck low. Arms protecting her head, she shifts forward and back, side to side.

"Kiko!" It's Jack—he throws Captain Maddie's cane high.

Amazingly, Kiko catches it as it twirls downward. She centers her weight, holding the cane like a bamboo sword.

"All the way across," orders Rattler. "Punishment for mutiny insubordination." He grins like a sleek hyena.

"Walk the plank, walk the plank."

Up high, the chant is more disorienting. Unbearably loud.

I step on the narrow plank. Kiko is a yard ahead. (Will the beam bear our weight?) I look up, then down. Above is a sky of artificial lights; below is packed dirt, cement, and flames.

I think of skyscrapers and graves.

Stones, skeletons fly. Rocks sail wide, especially from the younger boys. Others bruise my shoulder and arm.

Findley, aiming at my knees, is an expert. Tensing, I hope my legs won't buckle.

Kiko, with the cane, blocking, swinging, tries to defend us.

I want to run back to the landing. But now in the crow's nest, Rattler makes it impossible to retreat.

Running forward is dangerous, too. The beam only allows one foot forward at a time.

A rock hits my head. I lose balance; my feet swing out from under me, over the edge.

"Hold on, Zane."

My nails scrape into the plank. I gasp, grunting. Body weight strains my arms, hands.

Never-ending waves of stones, bones pass over me. Most hit my shoulders and back.

I'm not sure if I can save myself from falling.

I hear Jack cry, "You can do it, Zane."

Balancing, Kiko uses the cane to strike, deflect the missiles.

I adjust my grip, even though smaller stones sting like darts hitting my back.

Hip-Hop barks wildly.

"Walk the plank, walk the plank."

"You've got to be ready . . . Protect the bounty."

Captain Maddie?

I squeeze my eyes shut, and, muscles trembling, start to pull myself up. I—CAN—DO—IT!

"Protect the bounty."

"Defeat John," I murmur, trying to ignore pain. Ignore my worry that Kiko might be thrown off balance. Fall to her death. We both might fall to our death.

ONE . . . LAST . . . PULL.

Rage flows through me. "Captain Maddie!" I bellow, sweeping one leg over the plank, then the other.

Below, a hushed silence. John's frowning. No one throws anything.

Sitting upright, I look across at Rattler. I've never seen such rapturous fury.

Slowly, I stand. Younger boys below cheer. Like they've always been rooting for me. Like I'm a hero or something.

Bewildered, Kiko cries, "Let's get out of here."

One foot in front of the other. Foot by foot by foot. Much easier without stones and sticks being thrown.

We reach the end, the second crow's nest.

Boys clap as we climb down the ladder. Eyes sparkling, the youngest boys clamor.

"You knew Captain Maddie?" asks Devon.

"Of course he did." Jack pushes through the crowd. Boys part, make way.

Jack raises my hand like I'm a champion. (Or won a prize.) "He is Captain Maddie's first mate."

Younger boys clap, "ooh" and "aah."

Devon, Jace, the twins, and a dark-eyed boy press against me. "You knew Captain Maddie." "Really? You knew her?" "Where is she?" "I miss her."

"Where is she?" asks Devon.

Standing, I scan the tunnel. Rattler, Matt, and Findley have disappeared.

John looks—*what?* Shame-faced?

A tall, lean boy—one who favors Jack—asks, "Do you know if she's coming back?"

Me and Jack exchange looks.

Don't all the boys know she's dead?

"You didn't tell them," I holler, accusing John.

"Some of the older boys," whispers Jack, "know the truth."

The younger boys are filled with longing. A kid, tinier than Petey, tugs my shirt.

"This is Shawn," says Jack, scooping him up. "He's the youngest of them. The smartest, too." Jack tickles him; Shawn doubles over, laughing.

I marvel—Jack's the big brother.

"Me," begs another boy.

"You're too heavy." Jack squats, his arms wrapping about both boys. "Zane, this is my other friend. Lenny."

His eyes wide, the brightest blue, Lenny says, wistful, "Captain Maddie used to tell us stories."

I stoop, clasping Shawn's and Lenny's palms. Boys

huddle close. Dirty faces; shabby, ill-fitting clothes. I can imagine them loving Maddie. And Captain caring for her cabin boys.

Sad, I force a smile.

"Captain Maddie loved telling stories of seafaring, treasure hunting, derring-do. She told me lots. Now I can tell you," I say, gently poking Shawn and Lenny, "all the stories she told me."

Little ones cheer.

Jack nods approvingly.

"To Captain Maddie," I say, standing.

Kiko's cheeks are stained with tears. "And Captain Maddie's best first mate!"

"The best," hollers Jack.

I look at Captain John, whose face is closed, mysterious.

I grimace. Not once—not a single time—did Captain Maddie tell me about him.

Captain Maddie Was Here

Unbelievable. Captain Maddie was here. In these dank, foul-smelling tunnels. With Captain John and the pirate boys.

My mind hurts, my heart races.

I'm shaken. I thought I knew Captain Maddie. At least a little. She lived in our house for almost a year. I imagined her thrilling life at sea.

I never could have imagined her living here, in this depressing place, helping John mislead kids.

How could she even like John?

Of course she'd like him. Just like I did. (At least, at first.)

I sigh, resting my head on the tunnel wall. My back, shoulders, my entire body is sore.

I'm exhausted, fearful. Mourning that Captain Maddie's gone. Mourning for the boys who are still expecting to see her again.

No one guards me. Shouting "Captain Maddie" somehow eased suspicion. Even John ignores me.

(Maybe he's worried about Rattler, Findley, and Matt? Still no sign of them.)

Such a strange underground world—pirate emblems, fake rigging, and sails reflecting Christmas lights.

No longer chattering, the younger boys are curled in their hammocks, sleeping, dreaming. Of what— treasure? Golden coins? Jewels?

Scanning the bleak area, the empty hammocks, I can tell other, older boys have disappeared.

If this was a real ship, I'd guess some of the boys were mutineers. Rattler, their ringleader. Matt and Findley, thuggish lieutenants.

In my mind, I hear Captain Maddie: *"Watch for any strangers."*

I say out loud, "Especially seafaring men."

"Or boys. Seafaring boys."

Behind the drawn curtain, Petey groans. I think Kiko's applying more ointment, changing bandages.

Jack soothes, encourages, "You're a brave mate, Petey. I'm proud of you."

Hip-Hop, watching me, rests his head between his paws. I pet him, then close my eyes.

I'm not asleep. But behind my eyelids, I feel soothed by the darkness.

Hip-Hop growls.

Opening my eyes, I see John sauntering off-balance. Drunk? Knees bent, he lets his back slide down the wall.

"Yo, ho, ho, and a bottle of rum." He offers me his flask.

"Are you serious?"

He shrugs. "Rum cures a lot of ills. Course it's only allowed for officers. Like Rattler, Findley."

Anger chokes me. John lies. Worse, he's hurting kids.

John swallows, smacks his lips, and nudges me. "I didn't mean what I said. About you being whiny. A mama's boy. You're great. Anyone would be proud to have you as their son."

Just a bit, my anger lessens. John's charming me again.

I don't want to be charmed.

"Were you ever a pirate?" I demand. "A real one?"

Lowering his chin to his chest, he mutters, "No."

"Was Captain Maddie?"

"Yes."

I exhale, realizing I'd been holding my breath.

"Captain Maddie sailed everywhere. She came to Manhattan to hunt for the *North Star* treasure."

"You knew the whole tale?"

"Just bits, Zane. Not the entire story."

Turning, face-to-face, I ask, "Who are you?"

"A thief. Someone who thought they could outwit the great Captain Maddie."

"You sent the black spot?"

"Yes, you see, she'd figured out where the treasure was. But refused to tell me." Suddenly quiet, he sips from the flask. "Mind you, Maddie was always antique hunting, going to yard sales and flea markets. She read obituaries, visiting the grieving relatives. Said, 'Most misjudge the treasures they've got.'"

Like a silent film scrolling, I see Captain Maddie in an attic. She's searching through boxes, sorting papers, opening chests.

A girl with hoop earrings leans against a wall, bored.

Captain Maddie unsnaps a trunk's brass lock. Opening the lid, her hands hover, tremble. She lifts out a cane with a handle of twin snake heads. She tilts the cane upward, judging its weight, balancing it on her hands.

She peers into the chest again, plucks out a ring.

The girl extends her palm. Captain Maddie adds a twenty, then another, then another.

"The cane held the map. The girl didn't know."

"I didn't know," snarls John. "I suspected. But Maddie said the girl's grandfather lost a leg like some ancient pirate. . . ."

"Jambe de Bois?"

"Yes, that's it. 'Not from adventure. From diabetes.'"

"She grew more and more secretive." Jaw tightening, eyes fierce, John pokes me. "She betrayed me. We had an agreement." He gulps rum. "'A change of heart,' she said. A lousy, she-pirate change of heart."

Click-click: thoughts explode. Captain Maddie died in misery, hiding from John. Poor, like Ma, like all our boarders; nonetheless, she refused to share secrets about the treasure.

"Captain Maddie asked me, 'Is it more loyal to be disloyal?'"

"Did she now? Her disloyalty broke my heart."

"How? You aren't even a pirate. Not someone worth being loyal to."

He winces, covering his heart with his hands. "That hurts, Zane-boy. Captain Maddie gave me her word she'd share."

"Something else mattered more."

"I see why she liked you, Zane-boy."

"Stop calling me that!"

John chuckles. "See. You see me, all sides of me. Just like Captain Maddie did. I believe she loved me."

"Did you love her?"

John doesn't answer. "Before she left, she gave me this ring," he says, twisting it. "A goodbye parting. She didn't say so, but I suspected. As if it would be enough," he scoffs. "A reminder."

"The two-headed snake."

"Reminding me, her, of who I was. Holding the cane's snake heads, she said, 'I'll remember who I am. How we're the same.'"

A traitor? Liar? I remember: *Two-faced.*

"Petey's okay." Kiko halts when she sees John.

"Aw, Miss Kiko."

"Stop calling me that!"

Standing, unsteady, John pretends to sweep off a hat, and bows. "I've long admired you, Miss Kiko."

"NOT ditto! I don't admire you," she snaps. "What happened to your accent?"

John scowls. "You always make me angry. Almost as angry as Captain Maddie did."

Protect the bounty.

I reach my hand in my back pocket, touching the skeleton key. It's a key made for a door.

I stand up, tall as I can, but still only as high as John's chest. "We're not going to join you. You need to let me and Kiko go."

"Mind you, this means no treasure."

I clutch John's arm and, straight-faced, lie. "You've won. I've given up finding the treasure."

More than one of us can be two-faced. "Let us go. Me and Kiko just want to go home to Rockaway."

Quiet, John stares at my hand like it's foreign, odd. As if he's not used to getting touched.

"I appreciate your offer. At heart, I'm just not a pirate."

Jack pushes past the curtain.

"You leaving, too, Jack?"

"No," he answers, startled. "You leaving, Zane?"

"Yes. Going home."

"Zane, what're you—?"

I wave Kiko away, staying fixed on John's face. He looks woeful, weary. His eyes are dull. How come I didn't notice the deep wrinkles scoring his face?

"Do it. Leave." His face transforms. Sparks light his eyes; he grins wide. He's the familiar John again, chest puffed, voice confident and booming. "I'll find the treasure."

Unable to stop myself, I ask, "Did the younger boys know you gave Captain Maddie the black spot?"

"No, they loved her," he answers, his gaze deadening. "Me, I don't love anybody."

(I don't believe him. His strained voice makes me think he loved Captain Maddie.)

"Keep to the southeast," says Jack. "Eventually, you'll find a railing, a manhole for a safe exit."

"I'm going to miss you, Jack."

He shakes his head. "The younger boys need me. Maybe I can tell bedtime stories like Captain Maddie."

We clasp hands, lean in for a hug. Jack exhales a long sigh.

"You can change your mind, Zane-boy. Stay."

"No," I say, dropping my arms, letting go of Jack. "Come on, Kiko. Hip-Hop?"

Hip-Hop pushes through the curtain door, dragging the backpack.

"Wait." Serious, John warns, "Watch out for Rattler. He thought Captain Maddie made younger boys soft. Thought I was soft for living with her in our underground harbor.

"I may be two-faced. Rattler's not. Ruthless, he hates. Do you understand?" He pauses. "Betrayal is his middle name."

28

What's This?

Me and Kiko move silently, tiptoeing between hammocks and sleeping, snoring boys.

John leans against the wall, one foot propped, pretending not to watch. Jack, I know, will keep watch until he can't see us anymore.

"I can't believe you, Zane. You're giving up the treasure hunt?" whispers Kiko.

"Sssh. I've got a plan. Get our boards," I answer, pointing at the stack lining the wall. "Some flashlights, too."

I grab my board, matches, a torch. Secretly, I stuff two sticks of gunpowder into my belt.

We exit, turning east down a darkened tunnel.

Rattler, Matt, and Findley separate like shadows from the wall. Flashlights click on.

"What's this?" asks Rattler, holding the light beneath his chin. His white hair and sharp features seem ghostlier. "Escaping?"

"Captain John said we could leave."

"I don't believe you. Let's ask him."

Matt and Findley shove me and Kiko forward. Rattler quickly moves ahead yelling, "Captain John? Yo-ho, ahoy! Ahoy, Captain John."

Everyone wakes. The younger ones chatter excitedly while the older boys watch, wary and intent.

Feet up, John reclines in his leather chair. Behind him stands Jack.

"I found these two escaping," Rattler boasts. A few boys clap as he preens.

Captain John, focused, no longer seeming drunk, stands before Rattler. "They're not escaping. I told them to go."

"Is this true?" exclaims Rattler, betrayed. "What if they call the police? Like you said? What if they steal the treasure?"

"They won't."

Rattler reddens. "It's him," he says, pointing at Jack. "He made you change your mind. It isn't fair."

"What do you care about fairness?" I ask.

Rattler shoves me.

Jack steps between us. "Watch it, Rattler."

"You think you're special. I'm first mate and always will be." Turning to John, he pleads, "Jack's going to mutiny. He must've made a pact with his friends. They're going to try and steal the treasure."

"Not true. Zane-boy gave me his word."

"You believe the likes of him? And him—Jack? He's a spy, tricking you."

Menacing, John murmurs, "Are you saying I don't know best?"

Rattler steps back; John pushes forward; Rattler steps back again. John presses closer, towering over Rattler. But Rattler doesn't give another inch.

Everyone's quiet, breathless.

"That's it, Rattler. This is my ship, my harbor. I'm making Jack first mate."

Scornful, Rattler replies, "I demand a duel."

The boys gather, murmuring, shuffling, encircling John and Rattler.

"A duel," announces Matt. "It's a first mate's right."

"A battle among rivals?" muses John, then turns to me. "On your honor, Zane, swear you won't go to the police."

"I swear." (Knowing I will break my word.)

John decisively says to his crew, "Either way, Zane and Kiko are still free to go. But if you lose, Rattler," he says more quietly, "Jack becomes my first mate."

Rattler scowls.

"You didn't think you're first mate for life, did you? Competition is always good."

"I can beat him. Beat anyone," promises Rattler.

"Cocky," mutters Jack.

Everyone's eager—excited, enthralled.

Captain John stands between Rattler and Jack. Me and Kiko each place a reassuring hand on Jack's shoulder.

Rattler's friends, Matt and Findley, nervously shuffle behind him.

"Since letting Captain Maddie escape," Rattler says bitterly, "you've become a soft captain, John. But you"— his fist juts at Jack—"will never be first mate."

"Duel, duel, duel," the crew chants.

Jack glares at Rattler. "Bring it. If you dare."

Rattler's face twists. (He's uglier than I've ever seen him.)

"Quiet," commands the captain. "Is the duel accepted?"

"Accepted," says Jack.

"Man your boards," commands John.

Rattler has his. A sleek pro's board with a black maple deck and 75mm Orangatang wheels. Perfect for racing. (I'm sure it's stolen.)

Jack grabs his board near the tunnel's entrance. Like me, he bought the "best value" board at Big 5 Sporting Goods. It's not going to win any prizes. Except when steered by Jack. He's Rockaway's best. Always has been.

Boys clear an aisle for Rattler and Jack to walk toward the back. Me, Kiko, and Hip-Hop follow.

Captain John veers left, into another unfinished tunnel. "The dueling field!"

Matt switches on a portable generator. Balloon lights—like the kind used for nighttime construction—brighten the tunnel like daylight.

Amazing! My jaw drops. They've created their own park! A skate bowl with ramps, steps, and platforms. But it's the huge tunnel surface that's intimidating with its arcs and height. Fast, dangerous.

To sail here, you need helmets, elbow and knee pads. They still might not keep you safe.

Jack's shadow elongates. He's intense, his foot on his board, studying the park. His eyebrows pinch together above his nose.

Rattler bounces on his toes, throwing punches. (Seriously?)

"No one outskates me," he swears.

Captain John strides toward the skate bowl's heart. "Turbulent sea," he roars, turning. "Turbulent, underground sea. Aboveground," he proclaims, "the world is too staid, civilized. The waters, calm. But here, we're free! Everyone with a board, their own skiff to outsail, outmaneuver, outrace any challenger.

"The best two of three, mind you, crowns the champion. My new"—he looks at Jack—"or my old"—he looks at Rattler—"first mate.

"The crew decides the winner!"

Boys cheer; some squat, some sit cross-legged; others stand, excited and thrilled.

"Flip a coin for who goes first?" asks John.

Jack shakes his head. "Naw, I'll go first."

(Rattler's surprised.)

"Okay by you?"

Rattler blinks; his hand spasms. For the first time, I think he's anxious.

Knees bent, Jack pushes off with his right foot. He skates, cruising around ramps, low side-angling on walls, testing surfaces, then picking up speed. He rolls up the sides of the tunnel, higher and higher until he's almost horizontal to the floor. *Bam*, he does an aerial flip, then coasts up and down the sides, before landing with a kickflip.

"That's it, Jack! Go!"

Boys are screaming; some shout, "Show him, Rattler. Show him! You got this!"

Jack grins, knowing he did good. The kickflip was the cream on top.

Rattler's turn. Grimacing, he sails off. Wheels *whizzzz . . . whizzzzing.*

"Impossible," shout Rattler's lieutenants.

Impossible—one of the hardest tricks ever.

Rattler's in ollie stance, his front foot positioned

comfortably. His back foot, centered over the tail, presses down. His foot's inside edge scoops, making the board rotate.

Rattler's knees come up; his feet out of the way finish rotating and leveling out. As the board hits ground, his left foot steadies it, and his right foot kicks, and coolly, unbelievably, impossibly, he sails away.

Rattler nailed it! Worried, I look at Jack.

Jack's focused on his next trick.

Captain John yells, "Who won round one? Rattler?"

Shouts, especially from the older boys.

"Or your new mate, Jack?"

Clapping, cheering, screaming. The younger boys are rooting for Jack.

"Score a point for Jack."

Rattler curses, lurches toward Jace, sitting on the sideline. Jace flinches, falls against his friends.

Jack frowns, more determined to best Rattler. He kicks off. He's so at ease on his board, free sailing. He's not giving away which trick he has in mind. Instead, he's cruising, strategically unnerving Rattler.

"Do it already," Rattler hollers.

"Do it, do it, do it" resounds. Everyone chants. Jack stays cool, rising higher and higher on each side.

(He's going to do a frontside air.)

Jace screams, "Beat him, Jack."

"Beat him, beat him," others repeat.

Jack's in the air, his body vertical. His legs and board, right angled. His hand grips the board.

Gasps. "Whoa, way to go, Jack," "Terrific," "Super," the younger boys call out.

Jack repeats the trick. Yet instead of landing and stopping, he aims for a ramp. Unbelievable: one more trick.

I can tell Jack's planning to hit the ramp hard, sail down, scooping up the back tail into a hard stop. Before his wheels touch down, Rattler's board flies out from his feet. Jack's board is knocked sideways. Suspended in the air, he flails, falling hard. Instead of rolling, he extends his right hand.

"No!" I shout.

His slams on concrete.

Kiko rushes forward to help Jack.

"Cheat, cheat, cheat," I yell, pushing Rattler.

We scuffle. Captain John forces us apart, saying, "It's allowed. Pirates use every trick."

Outraged, I holler, "That doesn't make sense. Ask the others. Ask the crew." I look around—seeing the younger boys intimidated and the older ones gleeful. "Not fair."

John shrugs. "Fair is for landlubbers."

"It's okay, Zane," says Jack. "A tied score. I'll beat Rattler on the next round."

"You wish." Rattler pokes Jack's arm.

Jack winces.

"A sprained wrist, maybe," says Kiko.

I face Rattler. "I'm Jack's second."

Rattler laughs.

"I'll duel. It's allowed, isn't it? A sailor to take another's place."

"No, Zane, I can do it. I'll be all right." Jack tries to pick up his board; grimacing, he drops it.

"You can't skate!" Fierce, I look at Captain John. "Well?"

Quizzical, John studies me. "Never been done before."

"Let me try. Isn't that right, boys? Let me try."

"Let him try," yells Jace. "Yeah," Devon crows, "let him try." Others rally, chant, "Let him try, let him try, let him try."

Rattler holds up a hand. "It's okay. I can beat Zane. He's no pirate. He's a loser."

"I'll allow Zane to second Jack," says John, decisive. "If Zane wins, Jack is first mate."

"I won't lose. Zane-boy will. I've seen him fall before."

"Don't let him inside your head," cautions Jack.

I should be scared. Rattler's a much better skateboarder than me. But, looking at Jack, I know I have to win this for him. I forgive him for being a pirate. He's still one of my best friends.

Rushing forward, Kiko hands me a helmet.

"Thanks."

"Let's get on with it," Rattler hollers, scornful. "The duel!"

"Duel, duel, duel. . . ." voices clamor.

"You've got this, Zane," calls Jack.

"Thanks, Jack."

Rattler's boasting, tearing me down with his bullying mates, Matt and Findley.

"I'll go last," I say.

"Of course you will," scoffs Rattler, positioning himself on his board.

"Begin!" orders Captain John. "Last sail for the prize!"

Rattler's an expert sailor. Lean, dressed in black with shocking white hair, he looks impressive even to me. A cool villain.

He's sailing, *whizz-whizzing* along the bowl's bottom. Taunting me. Showing me his angles and glide. His smooth, effortless sailing.

Focusing on breathing, I try to calm myself. Jack slaps my back. Kiko grips my hand.

Spiteful, Rattler flashes me a nasty look. Then he leans forward, his back tightening, his leg kicking, pushing, picking up speed. He does a hardflip, the board spinning laterally while he jumps in the air. He speeds in circle eights, then does Jack's failed grind-and-slide trick down the rail, perfectly. Speeding again, he swings like a pendulum up, down across both sides of the bowl. Liftoff! Riding high, he grips his board with both hands.

Cheers explode! Three hard tricks strung together beautifully.

Rattler smiles, hands tapping his chest, shouting, "Beat that, loser!"

Strange, Captain John's behind me. Kiko and Jack are on either side of me. It reminds me of when I thought we were all united searching for treasure. Still a team.

I swallow, knowing I've never been as good a skater as Jack. What if I just fail again?

"Channel Hip-Hop," encourages Jack.

"Yes," says Kiko, scooping up Hip-Hop. "He's nimble, fast." Hip-Hop licks her face.

My stomach unknots. "Friends forever?"

Jack nods.

Kiko answers, "Don't even ask."

My board isn't the best, but it's familiar. Mine.

I hear the younger kids cheer: "You can do it," "Beat him," "Skate tough."

"Steer true."

I pause, step off my board, searching for Captain Maddie.

"Scared?" hollers Rattler, peering at me with contempt, like he did at Rockaway Skate Park.

But I won't let him make me feel small. Captain Maddie believed in me.

I study the bowl—the concrete planks, steps, concave sides. A turbulent, underground sea.

Click-click. My mind visualizes the tricks. *Focus on the horizon.* Where I'm going. Place to place. Trick to trick.

Do it. (Don't second-guess.)

Set sail. I kick, a slow, even pace. Slightly faster. Faster, faster. Fast. Faster than I've ever skated before. My wheels spinning, *whizzing*, drown out the crowd. I feel out-of-body, focused on the outcome, soaring up, then down the bowl's sides.

First, the ollie grab—the trick I failed in Rockaway. *Sail.* Crest the wave.

Focused, knees sucked up to my chest, I feel the forceful air helping stick my board to my feet. I squat, touch the board with two hands. *Score.*

I steer the board toward the wall, front wheels, then back sliding down, pendulum sailing, back and forth, back and forth between the walls. Next, I inhale, steer, kick hard up the ramp, then ollie down seven steps of concrete stairs. My feet, body, and board are like one, sailing the wave. I hard stop on the flat.

Boys roar. Kiko screams. Jack whistles, loud, sustained. Hip-Hop howls wildly.

I need to match Rattler—three outrageous tricks instead of one. I kick off, pendulum skating again between the tunnel's sides.

At the apex, I heel kick the board. It flips; I flip. Matching somersaults! I've never landed it. But I feel Captain Maddie's spirit sailing with me.

My heart pounds. One more.

Roll back down the wall and sideways stop with a flourish!

A happy, joyful noise erupts. Captain John claps. Jack's calling, "So dope."

I unbuckle and lift off my helmet. It was the perfect run. I couldn't have done it alone!

Rattler leaps toward me, swinging his board at my head.

Kiko shouts, "No!" parrying his board with hers, knocking it out of his hands.

"Tie him up," demands John.

No one moves. Rattler's crew shuffle, study the ground.

Stepping closer, Jack glares at the crew. "Tie Rattler up! That's an order from your captain. And your first mate."

Sketchy, shamefaced, Matt and Findley shift their loyalty from Rattler to Jack. Just like that!

Betrayal and Betrayers

I should be celebrating. Everyone else is—laughing, singing, eating, dancing jigs in the tunnel decorated like a concrete ship.

I sit, cross-legged, staring at the so-called dueling field, a mock concrete sea. Hip-Hop sits between my legs while I stroke his fur.

"Hip-Hop, why'd I help Jack become first mate?"

He tilts his head, his brown eyes looking at me.

"Friendship. Dad said, 'Disloyalty's always wrong.'"

But Jack isn't who I thought he was.

Comforting me, Hip-Hop licks my hand.

Jack would rather live underground than in Rockaway. Leave family and friends for thieves, fake pirates. Maybe I didn't really see him for who he was?

Beyond the park, Captain John sings:

Safe and sound at home again, let the waters roar, Jack.
Safe and sound at home again, let the waters roar. . . .

High and low-pitched voices resonate, bounce off tunnel walls. John's bass carries the melody, and someone, a tenor, adds harmony. A few sing off-key.

The singing saddens me.

I should be happy. Amazingly, I did the best skating of my life. I was inspired, defending Jack. And Captain Maddie's spirit helped.

Still, I feel empty. "Nothing makes sense, Hip-Hop. How can Jack be happy? How can John?"

I didn't understand John either.

"Two-faced," he'd admitted.

"That's it." I squeeze Hip-Hop. "A face you see and one you don't."

Click-click: the second clue. *Beware. Two-headed snake.*

Trying to steal the treasure, pirates betrayed abolitionists.

Next Thomas Downing. Two-faced, he hid the treasure.

John. A fake pirate, a schemer. Two-faced, trying to recover the treasure.

Dying, Captain Maddie said, "Two-faced." Yet I thought she was the truest of them all. A real pirate who sailed the seas, hunting for treasure.

Did the young Captain Maddie steal? Terrorize people on the sea?

The older Captain Maddie told tales, mothered young boys, and was a friend to me.

When she had the chance to share treasure with John, she changed her mind. She broke the pirate code. She was disloyal to John. *Two-faced.*

Three centuries of betrayal.

"Is it more loyal to be disloyal?" Captain Maddie asked.

She was John's ally but, ultimately, his enemy.

"Hip-Hop, no such thing as a two-headed snake." She always kept the cane close and clutched the handle tight. But maybe, just maybe, the cane's ivory heads weren't about John? Maybe they reminded her that it was okay to have two faces? Like Thomas Downing— who saved runaways while feeding oysters to enslavers?

In my heart, I know Captain Maddie made the right choice.

She didn't deserve the black spot.

In my heart, I know lying to John about hunting treasure was the right choice. He didn't deserve real loyalty.

I can't let him get the treasure—no matter what!

30

Try, Try, Try Again

"Zane, I brought some food and water."

Hip-Hop's tail wags, his body shimmies as he gulps chicken.

"Thanks, Kiko."

"You okay?"

"Treasure hunting isn't what I thought it would be."

I look out over the tunnelscape.

"It's like a sea," I say, pointing. "See how the ramps, their curves, seem like currents. The tunnel sides are like cresting waves."

"Or maybe a tsunami?"

"Yeah. I'm drowning in it. The treasure is somewhere above us, lost in the destroyed burial ground." I swallow. "But it's wrong to disturb graves, unearth bones."

"It dishonors the spirits."

"I think that's what Captain Maddie believed." (I want to confess I sometimes *hear*, *see* Captain Maddie.) Instead I say, "John's got to be stopped."

"So, you're not giving up?"

"No, it's *our* treasure. Not John's."

Hip-Hop slurps water. Kiko pours more into a cup. Hip-Hop drinks and drinks. I feel bad—he must've been dehydrated as well as hungry.

Water? I frown, remembering: *"Listen.*

"Water shows the way."

Excited, I pace. My mind reels.

"What are you thinking, Zane?"

I spin back around. "I followed the clues. But not all of them were written down!"

"There was a treasure map."

"Yes, telling and retelling a story, starting with runaways and gold."

"Gold meant for the underground railroad. The Black community."

"That's right, Kiko. When Captain Maddie found the map, there wasn't room to write another clue. But before she died, she told me, 'Listen. Waterfall. Tears.' It's got to be a clue."

"Waterfall? There aren't any underground water-falls."

"She was having a stroke. She slurred. What if she meant 'Water falls'? *Water* is *a guide*. A clue, a signpost."

"Yes! She meant, 'Like tears. Water falls like tears.'"

"Hey," calls Jack. "Captain John sent me to search for you two."

"Should we tell him?" asks Kiko.

"Tell me what?"

"Jack, this is going to sound strange—is there any water in these abandoned tunnels?"

"Yeah. John said southeast tunnels get filled with water. Sometimes from the rain, but also rotted pipes. New York City loses tons of water every day. There's seepage from sewers. Disgusting. Overflows from the North River."

Me and Kiko look at each other.

"What is it?" asks Jack. "You don't think I can be trusted?"

"Can you?" demands Kiko.

"Zane's always had my back. Maybe I was wrong to ally with John. But it wasn't about you, Zane. Or you, Kiko. It was about me."

"I never would've gone against you, Jack," I say.

"I know that. You're not as selfish as me. The duel proved it."

I blink, clutch Hip-Hop, worried I'll mistakenly trust again.

I decide: Jack's still Jack. My old friend. (But not for long.)

As if he heard me, Jack says, "I'll probably never see you again, Zane. Let me help. John doesn't have to know. What do you say? One last good memory."

I nod. Me and Jack high-five.

"Water is the final clue. John's exploding dry tunnels. He's on the wrong track."

"Whoa! Really?"

"And then there's this." My palm holds the black skeleton key.

We all stare at it—even Hip-Hop.

"This key means the treasure's in a chest, a trunk," Jack declares.

"Or behind a door. Look at its size."

Jack smiles, thrilled. "Sneak out. Get your boards. I'll distract John. Decoy, if need be."

"The original treasure hunters," I declare.

We clasp hands. Three mates. Three friends.

Kiko darts forward, hugs Jack.

"Ow, you're hurting me," he complains, grinning. Then says, "Keep sailing southeast. You'll hear water before you see it.

"I'll leave first. Create a diversion. Wait three minutes. Then go! Quiet, fast as you can."

I swallow, watching Jack skate, readying himself to betray John. (But not me.)

Placing a finger to my lips, I look at Hip-Hop. "Sssh. Be quiet. Just like we're sneaking down the stairs. Out of the house.

"Let's go!"

31

Onward, Sail On

Safe, beyond sight and sound of Captain John's harbor, we place our boards, kick off. *Whizzzzzzz,* our wheels scream through the channels of the sea. We keep sailing southeast. Keep turning to the tunnels on our left.

Gradually, then overwhelmingly, mud and puddles appear and rivulets of water spread, forcing us to walk. Tunnels sound muted, less sharp and cold.

We stop.

Two unreinforced tunnels, side by side, head southeast. Like gargantuan sea monsters had blazed ancient parallel trails.

"Do you think it's safe?"

"Not sure," says Kiko. "Digging subways began in the late 1800s."

"What choice do we have?" I step inside the first tunnel, feeling like I'm entering a waterlogged grave.

Walking gingerly, water and mud sucks in and out of our shoes. Hip-Hop leads, sniffing and scratching the ground.

"If it collapses, no one will know we were ever here," Kiko says, shuddering.

"Listen," I say. "Listen."

Inhale, exhale. Our breathing is loud. Hip-Hop snorts.

I hear *tinkling, plopping* water, like droplets dripping from faucets. I hear scurrying, too. Creatures? What kind?

"This isn't the place," I say. "For a sailor like Captain Maddie, there'd be more water. I'm sure of it."

"We should hurry to the second tunnel. In case Jack fails distracting John."

Kiko dashes back. I jog, slip and fall in the mud.

Trudging on, I lose sight of her.

She screams.

I speed up. "Kiko?" She must've gone right into the second tunnel.

Another scream.

"Find her, Hip-Hop."

Hip-Hop dashes. I race, too, my flashlight's beam cutting through the dark.

"No, Hip-Hop! No!" Kiko's screeching. "Stop."

Her light shines on hundreds of rats. Rats squeaking,

running, crawling over one another. Frenzied, trying to escape.

In his jaws, Hip-Hop snaps rat after rat. Shaking his head, he breaks their necks. He's an efficient killing machine.

"Hip-Hop!" I shout. "Stop." He doesn't stop.

"Make him stop," urges Kiko, appalled.

"He's a rat dog," I answer, marveling. "I've seen him catch a mouse, a rat. But never attack a whole colony."

Single-minded, second by second, Hip-Hop grabs another rat. And another. And another.

"'He's doing what a rat dog does,' as Jack would say. Hear it? Water rushing, thundering. Hip-Hop's clearing a path."

Kiko clicks off her light. "I don't want to see."

I clutch her hand, guiding her.

Hip-Hop *has* made a path—but it's gross. Limp rats, blood. Rats scurry and escape. Crafty, efficient, Hip-Hop darts, dashes. Dead rats pile up.

"Think, Kiko, what would we do if Hip-Hop wasn't here? He's helping."

"I hate rats," she whimpers.

I chuckle. "So does my dog."

"Listen, Kiko. More water, can you hear it? A stream, maybe a waterfall?"

I shine my light high. Above us are rusted metal pipes, mesh fragments. We must be far beneath some decaying water or sewage system. Or maybe, over time, river water pressure mangled pipes?

Mud's everywhere. Our beams brighten damp, slick walls. "Dangerous," I say.

"We could turn back."

"No, we'll keep going."

We trudge, deeper and deeper, into the tunnel. The air becomes more like mist; the *swooshing* water sound grows louder and louder.

Beneath our feet, dirt is slippery, soggier. It's hard to stay balanced.

"Look." A section of the side wall is collapsed. Water forced a path, making a waterfall. It's strangely beautiful. I stoop, touching a pool of water that becomes a narrow stream running south.

"Where's the treasure?" asks Kiko.

Yes, where?

My eyes scan, searching for a sign. Nothing, not a thing beyond a dark, too-moist underground world.

Inhale, exhale. I close my eyes, remembering how only three days ago, Captain Maddie was vibrant, alive. And fierce.

Water shimmers, seeming to slow, gently fall into the pool.

I hear a whispery soprano:

Safe and sound at home again, let the waters roar.
Safe and sound at home again . . .

"Let the waters roar," I sing. "She's here."

"Who?"

"Captain Maddie."

The waterfall is translucent—shadows, shapes hover behind it.

"Dead don't stay dead. Honor the bones," she said, dying, finishing the tale. *"Water falls like tears."*

I dash, splashing through muddy water, hoping I won't sink. Drown.

"What're you doing?"

"There's a space," I shout. "Behind the water." I disappear.

I'm inside *the water—hearing disembodied voices, the excited murmurings of spirits from long ago.*

"Zane!" cries Kiko.

"Now we're safe ashore. . . ."

"Captain Maddie?"

Her face is before me, smiling, filled with joy. "Don't forget your old shipmate. . . ."

"This is amazing," says Kiko, stepping into the alcove with Hip-Hop.

A cool, hazy mist cloaks all of us. I stretch out my arms.

"A door," I breathe. "A wooden door."

Our trembling hands explore the broad door with black metal braces, a knob, and a lock.

"The Sankofa sign," says Kiko, her finger tracing, "branded into the wood."

"We found it." Holding my breath, I insert the key into the lock and turn.

Our flashlight beams crisscross the small room, lighting several chests overflowing with gold coins.

"It must be worth millions."

Gold candelabras and gold chains are scattered throughout the room, on the floor, and on top of closed chests. Mirrors with elaborate gold filigree reflect more and more gold. Gold-cast tableware, flatware, and centerpieces decorated with gold-carved flowers and fruits form a large mound.

"Look," exclaims Kiko, holding open a jewelry box filled with gold rings, earrings, and necklaces studded with rubies, diamonds, and emeralds.

"We did it, Kiko!" I shout, plunging my hands into a gold pile, then abruptly lifting them.

Gold coins explode—twisting, twirling in the air, *clinking* together, sliding through my hands, back into the chest. Again and again and again.

Kiko coos. Hip-Hop barks.

I plunge my hands again. Gold reaches above my elbow. I've proved myself.

Captain Maddie hovers.

"Look, Kiko. Do you see her?" *Beams shine through a transparent shape.*

"Who?"

I exhale, feeling proud, happy.

"I miss you, Captain Maddie."

Her ghostly arms spread wide. A choir of whispery voices swell. "Safe ashore," they sing.

Captain Maddie beckons.

The world no longer feels upside down. Anxiety, fear, and sadness have drained. I appreciate Captain Maddie's smile. Dead, she's no longer cranky. Just a captain caring about her first mate and her crew— Kiko, even Hip-Hop. A captain caring for her dead passengers—runaways, city slaves, and free Blacks.

I feel a wave of warmth flooding over and through me. Behind the captain are rows upon rows of infinite spirits.

My heart soars. Captain Maddie's spirit, like my dad's, will always be a part of me. The tour guide spoke of honoring ancestors. Sankofa.

"The past isn't dead," I breathe.

The captain waves, follow me.

"Come on, Kiko." We twist, turn down passageways. *Captain Maddie guides.* (Hip-Hop walks beside her.)

"Where are we going, Zane?"

"Wait. Wait for it."

Captain Maddie stops, tilting her head back, and points.

"A manhole, Kiko! A way to escape John!"

"How'd you know it was here?"

"A special spirit," I say.

Our flashlights shine on the round metal door, the metal ladder that leads up and down from it.

"Let's go." I lift Hip-Hop, climb with one arm. Kiko's behind me. I hand-off Hip-Hop, and with all my strength, turn, turn, turn the stubborn, heavy wheel.

"Help," I murmur.

Voices grow louder, repeating, *"Safe ashore, safe ashore." The dead flood the room.*

Captain Maddie's hands embrace mine.

One last twist, I think. The handle turns; the manhole cover slides aside.

"We've done it!" Sunlight floods downward. Gold coins, gems sparkle.

I climb out, singing, "Safe and sound at home again . . . Let the waters roar."

Kiko hands me Hip-Hop. He struts in the fresh air, rubs his back on grass. We're at the edge of a small waterfront park.

I reach for Kiko, singing:

Safe and sound at home again, let the waters roar.
Now we're safe ashore.

As we slide the manhole cover closed, a spirit voice soars:

> *Don't forget your old shipmate.*
> *Faldee raldee raldee raldee rye-eye-doe.*

"Never!" I promise, hiding once again the precious treasure.

32

Pieces of Eight

The treasure was worth over fourteen million dollars! Our home was saved. It was part of my reward for finding the treasure. (Dad would be proud.)

I bought a new skateboard, too. Ma put the rest of my money in a college fund.

Kiko bought a skateboard and a boat. Sometimes, we just sail; other times, we go oystering. She has a college fund, too.

Hip-Hop got a new collar, stuffed rats to torment, and a soft bed.

New York City said the gold rightfully belonged in a trust for the African Burial Ground National Monument. Forever and ever, the past will be remembered and the ancestors honored. They've even created an exhibit, *Discovering Hidden Treasure* with statues of me, Kiko, and Hip-Hop.

At the opening ceremony, John stands off to the side,

still wearing his bell-bottom pants, gold chains, and billowy white shirt. His face drawn, joyless.

(He beams, though, when I approach).

"Zane-boy! My old mate. What ho?" he asks, rubbing his palms.

"How're you?"

"Never better," he boasts. "New adventures. New treasures to find."

Sadly, I don't believe him.

"How's Jack?"

"Best first mate a captain could ask for!"

I turn to go.

"Stay awhile." His hand brushes my sleeve.

Silence falls between us. The day is sunny; the air, fresh. Trees shade. I shiver, remembering John's underground ship.

"I did try to do right by you," says John.

"I know. You let me and Kiko go." But the price was for me to lie. Now I understand why Captain Maddie felt guilty not so much for betraying John, but more for betraying her own moral code.

"Zane." John rests his hand on my shoulder. "You didn't tell the police about me."

"Kiko argues omission isn't *exactly* a lie."

"Ah, smart, Miss Kiko." Then he whispers, "There's a bond between us. Isn't there, Zane-boy?"

I defended him. Looked up to him. Learned from him. My eyes moisten. *I will not cry!*

"Was, John," I say. "*Was* a bond. I look after myself now."

He pulls back, then nods. "I brought this for you." He hands me Captain Maddie's cane. "The map is still inside. Maybe the museum will find a use for it?"

"Thanks, John." I turn, abruptly stop and turn back. "John, did Captain Maddie have . . . did you and Captain Maddie really have a son?"

Captain John frowns, wrestling with some truth. He cocks his head, looks at me eye-to-eye, man-to-man. "No. She always wanted one."

My heart aches. One minute I'm happy; the next, sad. I grip the cane's ivory handle. Two-faced. Dual, dueling emotions.

"Don't think she lied to you!" John shakes me. "I wanted a son, too." He sighs. "Dying, Captain Maddie chose you as her son. She knew you'd never betray her."

"Zane!" calls Kiko, standing next to her parents and my mom. Hip-Hop barks.

"Winds are blowing us in different directions, lad." It's a statement. Nonetheless, I hear a lingering question— will we ever meet again?

John sounds more tender than I've ever heard.

Unable to stop myself, I hug him, clinging, smelling rum, feeling the press of his thick hands.

"Keep steering true, Zane."

"I will."

That was the end of it, the grand adventure. I haven't seen Captain John since.

33

The Story Ends

Nights, I sit on Captain Maddie's old bed. Legs twitching, snorting, dreaming of catching rats, Hip-Hop sleeps on the pillow.

Life is mostly good.

Ma doesn't have to take in boarders. She let Mr. Butler stay. (He makes her laugh.) She says, "You've changed, Zane. Before I know it, you'll be off to college. Out on your own."

I *have* changed. My feelings are as complicated as the ocean. Sometimes stormy; sometimes calm.

Except for me and Kiko, no one in Rockaway knows the full story of what happened in Manhattan. I told Jack's mom he was safe, happy. Skeptical, she said, "I hope he makes a home. Nothing for him here."

Afterward, upset, I hugged Ma ever so tight.

(I promise never to worry her again.)

Tonight, I stare out the bay window, watching the

waves, the white-sailed ships. Skyscrapers sparkling in the far distance remind me of the Christmas lights in the turbulent, underground sea.

I miss Jack. Some nights, I wonder if he's at the harbor looking across the water at Rockaway, thinking about me. Once, I stood at the open window, whistling, hoping I'd hear his answering call.

I sigh. "Come on, Hip-Hop. Let's skate."

His ears perk up and he leaps off the bed. This is our new routine. A nighttime skate, sailing by the brightly lit boardwalk, the skate park, and down to the sea.

"How about another adventure, Hip-Hop? Would you like that?" He plops, *thunk-thunk-thunk* down the stairs.

Though the journey was hard, it was thrilling. Unforgettable.

There's something special about a seaman's life— even if you're a pirate. I smile.

"Freedom. You're called to it, too. Aren't you?"

Captain Maddie, Jack, and Captain John will always be part of my story.

"Time for a new chapter."

With my friend and best dog, Kiko and Hip-Hop. (And who knows, maybe Jack?)

Zane's Skateboarding Trick Glossary

BACKSIDE POWERSLIDE: The skater swings the rear of their board forward so that the back and front wheels align and the board slides forward instead of rolling; the skater faces away from the direction that the board moves.

BOLD LANDING: A clean, solid landing after a trick.

BLUNTSLIDE: The skater pops their board up and slides along a rail, curb, or other surface using the tail of the board.

FRONTSIDE AIR: The skater launches into the air (usually from a half-pipe or skating pool wall) and grabs the middle of the board in front of them while in the air.

GRIND AND SLIDE: The skater scrapes the skateboard's trucks along a rail or other surface and slides as long as they can.

HARDFLIP: A combination of a kickflip and a frontside pop shove-it in which the board rotates along both its lengthwise and vertical axes.

HEELFLIP: The skater flips the board with their heel in the opposite direction of a kickflip.

HEEL SCRAPE: A way to brake; the skater pushes the back of the board down until it scrapes the pavement and brings the board to a stop; also known as tail drag.

IMPOSSIBLE: The skater begins in ollie stance. Their back foot, centered over the tail, presses down and scoops with the inside edge of the foot to make the board rotate. The skater's knees come up to let the board rotate and level out. As the board hits ground, the front foot steadies it so that the rear foot can push off.

KICKFLIP: The skater flips the board around its lengthwise axis using their front foot.

OLLIE: The skater uses their feet to pull the skateboard up into the air.

POP SHOVE-IT: Combines the ollie with the shove-it so the board goes into the air and rotates along its vertical axis.

POP UP: The skater pushes the back of the board down until it pushes against the pavement, bringing the nose up and making the board "pop" upward.

POWERSLIDE: The skater swings the rear of their board forward so that the back and front wheels align and the board slides forward instead of rolling; the skater faces the direction that the board moves.

ROLLING OLLIE: An ollie performed in motion (while rolling).

Afterword

Most of the details in this story are unfortunately true.

The Municipal Slave Market operated from 1711 to 1762 at Water and Pearl Streets in Manhattan. Enslaved Africans built the wall where they were chained and sold. They contributed to the development and economic engine of New York—clearing land, building city hall, prisons, hospitals, and premier buildings such as Trinity Church, Fraunces Tavern, and much of Wall Street itself. Historic narratives of how Black people contributed to New York becoming the economic heart of the world have been ignored or intentionally repressed. In the 1700s and 1800s, the enslaved population grew to well over a million.

Most early New Yorkers were anti abolition, given their strong ties with the cotton trade and shipping industry and their financial partnerships with banks and insurance companies. Almost half of white households owned servants and laborers. Despite this, New York was an important stop and way station for the Underground Railroad. Many of the runaways arrived in New York by boat, having bribed ship captains (both pirates and non-pirates). Multiracial crews (some themselves former enslaved people) welcomed

them and aided their transfer to Black and Indige-
nous oystermen, who sailed them in canoes across
the harbor to shore.

Thomas Downing, the son of enslaved people, became
"the Oyster King" and was so beloved that when he
died, the Chamber of Commerce closed Wall Street
on a weekday. White businessmen who had dined at
his elegant, segregated restaurant wanted to attend
his funeral.

Downing, though, lived a double life. His wealth
funded the Underground Railroad. He hid runaways
in his basement, while above, politicians, captains of
industry, and the police roamed the streets and dined
in his restaurant. He was a tireless supporter of the
entire Black community, including funding the African
Free School for youth.

Downing would've been buried in the six acres des-
ignated as the African American cemetery. Over time,
this cemetery became valuable land to build upon.

The National Historic Preservation Act of 1966
mandates a cultural survey of federal building sites.
In 1991, while preparing to build a new office at 290
Broadway, the largest known African American burial
ground in North America was discovered. The African
American community rallied for preservation and honoring of the forgotten ancestors. One-sixth of an acre

was set aside for the African Burial Ground National Monument. Fifteen thousand intact skeletal remains were discovered, and bones were found as deep as thirty feet. The rest of the original colonial cemetery acreage had been built upon and rebuilt upon. In the museum today, there is a chart illustrating three centuries of differing historic foundations that have been layered over coffins. How many more bodies are buried beneath Lower Manhattan buildings? How many times were bones and skeletons discarded to make way for construction?

Updating *Treasure Island* was a pleasure. Manhattan is the perfect island for modern skateboarding pirates. Particularly during the pandemic, young people embraced the freedom of sailing with skateboards. Rockaway and New York City experienced an explosion of skateboard culture.

Historical fiction is a combination of accuracy and fictional lies. But, always, the intent of fiction is to tell the emotional truth of characters journeying through life.

My Rockaway is a nostalgic beach town with a carnival boardwalk that is welcoming for kids. This contrasts with the harsh realities Zane, Jack, and Kiko experience in New York City. So, moving from a more innocent atmosphere of my imagined Rockaway intensifies the characters' stakes and self-discovery in a harsher, less child-centered New York City.

Robert Louis Stevenson's *Treasure Island*, published November 14, 1883, is an engaging, imaginative story of derring-do and pirate lore. The emotional core of the book is the crisis of Long John Silver, an adult, betraying a child. Such betrayal was a radical notion in the Victorian era, when children's literature primarily depicted adults as moral and ethical role models. Adults civilized children. Adults didn't lie.

The heart of my book, *Treasure Island: Runaway Gold*, focuses on the emotional disturbance of Captain John's betrayal. As in Stevenson's novel, the hero's heartbreak is made more intense by having lost his father. Zane, vulnerable, looking for a father's guidance and comfort, learns about adult hypocrisy and "two-faced" lies. Growing up is a necessary, bittersweet rite of passage for Zane. For all children. Some innocence is always lost.

Narrative style is important to me. I try to share with readers some of the resonance and rhythm of the African American oral tradition. Zane, through his voice, I hope, exemplifies a cultural voice as well as the intelligence and agency inherent in today's youth.

I also love writing about cross-cultural spiritual traditions. Many of the world's religions share beliefs in everlasting spirits and ancestor worship. African, African American, and Japanese Shinto religions echo one another in that the past informs the present and the future. Kiko, as a mixed-race child, Japanese and Black, embodies her father's culture and her mother's culture and profession of teaching Africana studies (the multidisciplinary study of Africa and its descendants in the Black diaspora). Captain Maddie's seafaring echoes this historical and ongoing Black diaspora and the New York–based trade of enslaved peoples.

I enjoyed writing *Treasure Island: Runaway Gold* very much.

I love my characters! Zane, Jack, and Kiko. What is life without good friends? And, finally, what would a story be without a dog? Yay, Hip-Hop!

Acknowledgments

Books are *always* collaborative efforts.

Special thanks to Petersen Harris and Alli Dyer of Temple Hill Publishing for inspiring me to retell *Treasure Island.* I had so much fun!

My amazing editor, Rosemary Brosnan, at Quill Tree Books expertly helped me to become a better writer. Her guidance and insights were superb.

Rosemary's HarperCollins colleagues graciously supported *Treasure Island: Runaway Gold* throughout its long journey through design and production and into bookstores and schools. I can't thank them enough for their work and belief in me and my revisionist tale. Thanks to: Suzanne Murphy, president and publisher; David Curtis, associate art director; Courtney Stevenson, associate editor; Shona McCarthy, senior production editor; Jacqueline Hornberger, copy editor; Mark Rifkin, executive managing editor; Patty Rosati, senior director of School and Library marketing, and her team; Kerry Moynagh, VP, executive director of children's sales, and her team; Robby Imfeld, marketing director; and Taylan Salvati, publicity manager; and Annabelle Sinoff, production assistant.

ACKNOWLEDGMENTS

Thanks to Raymond Sebastian for his terrific cover art and interior illustrations. His art truly uplifted my tale!

A hug to my agent, Michael Bourret, who helped make my dream to become a children's author come true.